'a really enjoyable read' SUNDAY TRIBUNE

'beguiling and engaging...should keep young
teenagers enthralled' THE IRISH TIMES

'compelling...will appeal to anyone who likes adventure'
THE ECHO

'a well-written and warmhearted story...
populated with the quirky and irrepressible'
ROBERT DUNBAR, CHILDREN'S BOOKS IN IRELAND

Special Merit Award to The O'Brien Press
from Reading Association of Ireland
'for exceptional care, skill and professionalism in
publishing, resulting in a consistently high standard in all
of the children's books published by The O'Brien Press'

ABOUT THE AUTHOR

Frank Murphy used to be a school principal who wrote whenever he had a moment – poetry, school books and short stories in Irish and English. When he retired he had time to write his first full-length novel, *Lockie and Dadge*. He followed this success with some books for younger readers – *Charlie Harte and his Two-Wheeled Tiger* and retellings of *Gulliver* and *The Táin*. When not writing or reading, Frank leads a quiet life in the countryside, just outside Cork, and likes to take unrestful holidays in cities.

Lockie and Dadge

Frank Murphy

Ⓑ

THE O'BRIEN PRESS
DUBLIN

First published 1995 by The O'Brien Press Ltd.,
20 Victoria Road, Dublin 6, Ireland.
Tel +353 1 4923333 Fax +353 1 4922777
e-mail books@obrien.ie
Website http://www.obrien.ie
Reprinted 1997, 1999

ISBN 0-86278-424-7

British Library Cataloguing-in-publication Data
Murphy, Frank
Lockie and Dadge
I. Title
823 [J]

3 4 5 6 7 8 9 10
99 00 01 02 03 04 05

Separations: C&A Print Services, Dublin
Printing: Cox & Wyman Ltd., Reading

Contents

CHAPTER ONE

Home, Sweet Home

It wasn't much of a place, a line of small grey houses. They all looked the same, only for the doors. The doors were different colours. Miss Cuneen stopped the car at a house with a brown door, and a black knocker and letter-box.

Clouds the colour of mud covered the sky, and it was twilight all day, as if the sun had turned its back. So it wasn't much of a day either.

Miss Cuneen said: 'Here we are. Number seventy-three. Out you get, Lockie.' She sounded cheerful, but Lockie knew that she just wanted to make him feel good.

She was a social worker with the Health Board and she was trying to find a good foster home for him. 'You'll have to be with someone who can teach you self-discipline,' she said, 'so that you'll grow up to be a responsible and valuable person.'

But all Lockie wanted was a place where he could feel at home. It didn't have to be posh or rich or anything like that, once he didn't feel like an outsider, a young cuckoo in another bird's nest.

Miss Cuneen spoke slowly and carefully. When she was

about to say something, she puckered her lips, as if she were going to whistle. That was to make sure that her words sounded right when she let them out for the world to hear.

'Here we go again, Lockie,' she said. 'Your third home in only five years. It's your last chance. I don't know what will happen if you don't settle down here.' She paused. She must have seen the bleak look in his eyes. 'The Farrells are very good people,' she went on, cheerful again, 'and I'm sure you'll get on like a house on fire.'

Lockie said nothing. What was the point? Miss Cuneen always said things like that, but it never worked out. But, she had touched on a sore spot. He was tired of being moved from one family to another, like a piece of furniture.

This time his mind was made up. He would be quiet. He wouldn't be any of the things his previous foster parents said about him: cheeky or stubborn or impossible. He had never really wanted to be any of those things anyway.

Miss Cuneen tripped up the narrow concrete path to the door and knocked. She looked neat and business-like in her smart red suit.

The door opened and Lockie's new 'mother' stood there. She wore glasses that reflected the light like a mirror, and Lockie couldn't see her eyes. He liked to be able to look into people's eyes, so he could get an idea of what they were thinking.

As he followed Miss Cuneen into the tiny hallway, he knew the woman was sizing him up. He could almost feel her eyes boring into the back of his skull.

'Is he still a handful?' she asked Miss Cuneen, as if Lockie were no more than a bag of potatoes, and deaf at that. It was the same in the other families. He didn't count. But he wouldn't let it get to him.

'Depends on how you treat him,' Miss Cuneen said sharply.

'Oh, you've no need to worry on that score. John and I are quite capable of dealing with high-spirited boys.'

'There are a few things you must remember.' Miss Cuneen spoke emphatically. 'Lockie was abandoned when he was very young. Who knows what effect that has had on him? Up to now he's lived in cities – with families in Dublin, and, lately, with a family in Cork. You're quite close to Dublin here, but at least he'll have a chance to look at the sea. I'm hoping a small town will suit Lockie better.'

The first few days in a new family were always tricky. Lockie had to discover their peculiarities, what they liked and what they didn't like. He had to know where was the line he couldn't step over. His trouble was that no matter what he did to please, he always seemed to get it wrong.

Lockie was keyed up, watching for signs in the way Rita Farrell spoke, the way she looked at him. Her glaring spectacles made it difficult for him to fathom her attitude.

Lockie's 'little sister', Ruthie, who was six, and his 'new brother', eight-year-old Gordon, were introduced. Gordon and Ruthie sat side by side, clean and washed, on the long sofa. They smiled non-stop.

Miss Cuneen and Mrs Farrell chatted for a while about things in general, and about Lockie in particular. His 'quick fuse', as Miss Cuneen called his fiery temper, wasn't mentioned. Then the time came for Miss Cuneen to depart, and Lockie was sorry to see her go. He was on his own now.

'Are you hungry?' his new mother asked him. 'You've had a long drive from Cork.'

'Yes.'

'Well, it won't be too long now until Mr Farrell gets home. We'll all have tea then. Meals in this house are at regular times. We don't have anything in between.'

'May we go out now, Mam?' Gordon asked.

'Yes, but first come along up to your rooms and we'll change your clothes.'

Lockie knew it. They had been putting on a show for Miss Cuneen. The clothes and the smiles were all for her benefit.

While the others were upstairs, he looked at the bookcase in the living-room. All the books were about the sea and sailing: *Two Years before the Mast, Mr Midshipman Easy, The Nigger in the Narcissus, Nautical Almanac, Mutiny on the Bounty.*

The others came downstairs, and Mrs Farrell sent them all out to play. The back yard was tiny, a triangle between the yards of two neighbouring houses. An apple tree took up most of the space.

'I know all about you,' Gordon said. 'You're wild.'

'Shut up!'

'You can't touch us,' Ruthie mocked. 'My Daddy said we were to tell him if you did. So there!'

They were much younger than him, so they could say what they liked. Lockie didn't care. They played their childish games 'Guess what I'm thinking about now' and 'I spy with my little eye'. Lockie sat silent, brooding, for over an hour on a solitary concrete block near the back door.

When John Farrell came home, they were called indoors. Ruthie and Gordon ran to him, shouting, 'Daddy, Daddy, look. Lockie is here.'

John Farrell was in a busman's uniform. He shook hands with Lockie and said, 'Welcome aboard.'

Lockie didn't know how to take him. He seemed pleasant enough, but Lockie had learned not to rush things in a new home. Still, he thought he might try to close the gap between them. Miss Cuneen had told him to do that.

'Hello, Dad,' he said, looking hard at John Farrell to see how he would react. Breaking down barriers, Miss Cuneen called it. Establish a father-son relationship from the beginning, she had advised.

'Well now, Lockie,' Rita Farrell chipped in, 'I think "Mr Farrell" and "Mrs Farrell" might be better than "Dad" or "Mam".'

John Farrell gave an embarrassed little laugh. 'After all,' he said, 'it's not as if you were with us from infancy. Babies don't come your size.' And he threw his head back and roared laughing as if he had made a wonderful joke. 'Anyway,' he continued, 'what I really want you to call me is "Captain". You say it, "Cap'n", like that. Like a real seaman. Okay, Lockie?'

'Okay.' So, the books must be his.

'Not okay, matey. You say, "Aye-aye, sir!" Real snappy. Like that. Go on, try it.'

'Aye-aye, sir,' Lockie repeated as snappily as he could. His new 'father' obviously wanted to be a sailor. Probably comes from living by the sea, thought Lockie.

They had tea. Ruthie and Gordon prattled on and on, but Lockie had nothing to say. After the meal, Rita said, 'You might as well get your hand in, Lockie. You can wash up this evening.'

Later, when John Farrell left the room, Rita said, 'Mr Farrell likes to run this house like a ship, and you must fall in with that.'

'Was he a sailor?' Lockie asked.

'Only for a short time. He had to give it up because he was always sea-sick. The ship's doctor advised him to get a shore job. That was awful for him because all his family were sailors.'

Lockie said nothing. He went to the kitchen and began to wash the dishes. Rita Farrell came to the kitchen door and said, 'Did you hear what I said, Lockie? You will fall in with his way of doing things, won't you?'

'Okay,' Lockie answered. If Mr Farrell wanted to play "Let's be sailors", why should he worry?

CHAPTER TWO

Fracas in the Playground

Lockie was glad when bed-time came. He took his bag up to the room he was to share with Gordon.

John Farrell snapped out orders as if he were briefing a crew before they went on watch: 'You take the top berth, Lockie. Gordon is not a good climber. This locker here is yours. Keep this room ship-shape at all times and don't forget your prayers.'

Lockie unpacked. When he had put his clothes away, he emptied his pockets and laid everything out on the locker. There was a key to somewhere, a piece of polished stone, a large glass marble with arabesques of red and orange in it that glowed like fire when you held it to your eye, a pen-knife, and, his most prized possession, a flashlamp lens which he used as a magnifying glass. Gordon came to look.

'What's that for?' he asked, pointing at the lens.

'For looking at things.'

'What things?'

'Dead flies and spiders and things like that.'

'And what do you want this for?' Gordon asked, picking up the knife.

Lockie snapped it out of his hand. Gordon was okay, a bit innocent, but if they were going to share a bedroom, it was time to lay down a few ground rules. 'Don't touch it, Gordon. If you ever lay a hand on any of my things you'll be sorry.'

Gordon opened his mouth wide. At first nothing happened. Then a sorrowful wail, loud and continuous, came from his gaping mouth. He showed no emotion, no tears, and his eyes were dead-pan. But that awful wailing sound, like a factory siren at knocking-off time, filled the room.

It stopped, and Lockie was relieved, but his relief didn't last long. Gordon was merely pausing to draw breath before beginning again, louder and at a higher pitch. You could see he was trying to get a message to his parents, and he succeeded.

Lockie could hear the thump of footsteps racing up the stairs. The door opened and Rita Farrell rushed in. Gordon ran to her and buried his face in her midriff. 'He's at me!' he wailed.

John Farrell arrived on her heels. 'What's going on?' he asked.

'I didn't touch him,' Lockie said.

'Then why is he crying?'

'I just told him to leave my things alone,' said Lockie.

'He said he'd kill me,' Gordon lied. 'I'm afraid to go to sleep. And he has a knife.'

John Farrell confiscated the knife, but that didn't satisfy Gordon. He refused to sleep in the same room as Lockie. Mr Farrell removed the mattress from the top bunk and made a bed for Lockie in the hallway downstairs.

'From now on, matey,' he said, 'you sleep on the main deck.'

Lockie lay awake for hours. He was furious at the injustice

of it all, and his good intentions evaporated. He kicked at the bed-clothes, and shouted, 'It's not fair!'

A bedroom door opened upstairs and John Farrell's voice called out, 'What's going on down there?'

Lockie didn't answer, but held his breath in the heavy silence. Eventually the door upstairs closed again. Lockie's anger left him then. In a strange way he was satisfied. His place in this family had been established, and they must have got some idea of the way he felt. There was no more uncertainty.

Yet sleep came slowly because he was trying to get his bearings among the night sounds in his new home: the ticking clock, chairs creaking, a cat scraping at the refuse bin outside the back door. It seemed as if he had just dropped off when he heard John Farrell shouting: 'Rise and shine! All hands on deck!'

'On deck! On deck!' Lockie said to himself. 'Where does he think he is? On the *Bounty*? Bloody Captain Bligh!' He smiled at the thought – he had a name for him now. Lockie set great store on naming things. When he had his own name for a thing or a person, he felt he had some secret power over them.

That day Rita Farrell took him to the local school.

'Let me see now,' his teacher Mr Bradley said when the headmaster had shown him to fifth class, 'where will we put you? Why don't you sit there with Mickey Wheeler.'

Lockie went to a desk at the back of the room. He could feel the eyes of the others on him as he took the chair beside Mickey Wheeler. Mickey was smaller than himself, and his jet-black hair tumbled over his forehead. He was dark-skinned, like a Spaniard or an Italian, and he smelt of wood smoke.

'Page thirty-six,' the teacher's voice broke into his thoughts. 'You read, Lockie, just to see where you fit in.'

Lockie could read well, and he read the page carefully. It was easy.

'Well done!' said Mr Bradley. 'Continue, Mickey.'

Mickey made a show of getting to his feet and of taking the book from Lockie.

'Where is it?' he whispered, and Lockie pointed. Mickey was a poor reader, slow and hesitant, struggling through word by word, with pauses between them and long pauses before the hard words. He stopped dead at 'furniture'. 'Tell me!' he whispered fiercely out of the corner of his mouth.

Lockie whispered the word, and Mickey blurted it out as if he had just that moment managed to work it out. 'Thanks!' he muttered as he sat down. They were friends now.

Playtime came, and all the classes surged into the playground. For Lockie it was the same old ritual. He kept himself to himself, standing with his back to the wall, staring at a point about two inches in front of his toes, and saying nothing.

From time to time he looked up and watched the others at play. The noise was deafening. A rabble of boys raced helter-skelter in all directions. They ran singly and in pairs, in threes or in squads of ten or twelve. Some of them were planes or birds, arms spread wide, hovering, banking, diving. Others pointed fingers and made gunfire noises. There were cowboys and Indians, kangaroos and horses, cars and buses, footballers, and high jumpers – a frantic, screaming mob.

Mickey was always last in a line, or on the fringe of a flurry, never at the heart of things. Spurned by one group, he trotted to another, and, a few minutes later, to yet another.

Lockie watched him. Why didn't he cop on? They didn't want him.

≋   ≋   ≋

At the Farrells Lockie was allowed back to the bedroom after four nights in the hall, and life became half-normal. On Sunday the family went for a stroll on the seafront. John and Rita walked ahead with the two younger children, and Lockie tagged along behind.

At the end of Cloughlee pier an old tall ship, *The Golden Albatross*, was moored. It had been restored to the glory of its sailing days, and was now a museum. Mr Farrell paid the entrance fee and they went aboard by the gangway. They spent an hour wandering around the polished wooden decks, and below deck they inspected the cabins and stores and the galley.

John Farrell could have got a job as the official guide, he knew so much about it. He named all the sails which were furled on the 'yards' and asked Lockie to repeat them. Names like 'main top gallant studding sail' and 'mizen topsail' fell from his lips as if he had come straight out of a sea story. Lockie found it interesting at first, but John Farrell went on and on, and it became boring.

≋   ≋   ≋

For a whole week life at school went on as it had on the first day. Lockie spent playtime standing by the wall. Mickey came and talked to him sometimes, but the other boys ignored him.

Then they began to taunt him. At first they ran very close by him. Then some of them grew bolder and brushed against him as they passed. One or two crashed into him. Then Jimmy Walsh, a small, blond boy with a wide gap in his front teeth stood before him, pointed a finger at him and shouted 'Mawface!' A crowd gathered round and joined in, chanting and clapping their hands, 'Mawface!' clap-clap-clap, 'Mawface!', clap-clap-clap.

Mickey Wheeler came and stood beside Lockie. 'Don't mind them,' he said. The chanting and clapping continued, and although Jimmy Walsh had started it, a tall red-haired boy from another class took over as the leader. He turned his back on Lockie and began to direct the others, like a band-conductor.

It was too much for Lockie. Good resolutions were forgotten. He dashed from the wall and dived at the red-head, catching him in a rugby tackle around the knees. The 'conductor' fell to the ground, and immediately a swarm of boys launched an attack on Lockie. He backed over to the wall and lashed out with both fists. For five minutes he was caught in a flurry of flying fists that landed like bee stings on his face and chest.

Mickey Wheeler stood shoulder-to-shoulder with him, battling away. Mickey was small but his arms moved almost as fast as the wings of a humming bird that Lockie had seen on a television programme.

The whole school gathered to watch the mêlée. Finally the bell went and the combatants disengaged and shuffled to their class line. Lockie's face was blotched with reddening bruises, and Mickey had a bloody nose.

'What happened here?' Mr Bradley asked, when he saw Mickey's nose.

'An accident, sir,' Mickey answered.

'They attacked other boys,' their classmates said in a chorus.

'Who did?' Mr Bradley asked crossly.

'Him and Lockie Farrell, sir,' the red-head shouted from the next line. 'They attacked Jimmy Walsh and other small boys, sir.'

He and Mickey were sent to the headmaster and detained after school. Gordon brought the news home to Rita, and John Farrell was given the story when he came in from work. Lockie insisted that it was not his fault, but they didn't believe him. He was sent to bed without anything to eat.

He lay on the bunk, thinking: This place is no better than the others.

It wasn't so much getting into a row with his schoolmates, or even being kept in after school. He could get over that, but the loneliness hit him, the feeling that he did not belong in this family, or in the school, or in the town, just like the other families and schools and towns where he'd been. Mickey Wheeler was the only friend he had.

CHAPTER THREE

The Last Straw

'What did they say to you?' Lockie asked Mickey next day at school.

'Who?'

'Your father and mother.'

'About what?'

'About being kept in.'

'They don't know anything about it. They weren't there when I got home.'

'The Farrells sent me to bed without my tea.'

'Why?'

'For being kept in.'

Mickey laughed. 'They're weird,' he said.

In the yard the other boys gave them plenty of space. Lockie knew it would be like that. Once you stood up to them, they wouldn't try anything again. He had seen it all before.

Mickey stopped trying to get into their games. He and Lockie spent playtime together. They moved away from the wall and ran about, or walked through the pandemonium, talking to each other. They talked about home, and the people they knew, and Mickey said he was a Traveller and told Lockie all about the way his people lived. Lockie talked about his foster homes and his new family.

Lockie told Rita he didn't have enough to eat at lunch time. 'You'll eat us out of house and home,' she said, but she gave him a few extra slices of bread. Lockie wanted them for Mickey. He had noticed that Mickey brought no lunch to school.

'What's it like living in a caravan?' Lockie asked him one day.

'It's okay. Come home with me after school and have a look at it.'

'When?'

'What would be wrong with today?'

'I have to take Gordon home, and I'm not allowed out after that.'

'Well, don't go.'

'They'd murder me if I let Gordon go home on his own.'

'Bring him home, but don't go in. They can't keep you in then.'

≈   ≈   ≈

Lockie had his own latch key. He opened the door and let Gordon in. When the door closed behind the younger boy, Lockie ran like a scared cat to join Mickey around the corner, and they raced all the way to the Wheelers' caravan. It was parked at the edge of town, on a straight stretch of the Coonmore road.

They went in. The table had not been cleared after breakfast. Cups containing the dregs of tea and with brown drips of tea-stain on the outsides, stood on the table. A half-cut loaf lay on its side in a scatter of crumbs and un-washed knives and spoons.

Mickey got an enamel basin and filled it with cold water from a bucket that stood in a corner. He washed the whole lot, and Lockie dried. Mickey then lit the gas stove and put a kettle on to boil.

'The small ones will be home soon,' he told Lockie, as he cut thick slices of bread from the loaf. He buttered the bread and left it stacked in the middle of the table.

The younger Wheeler children arrived shortly after that from the local convent school – three of them, Kitty and Molly and Tommy. They tucked into the bread and butter and tea. Lockie joined them. The caravan was small and crowded, and the food wasn't great, but the Wheeler children didn't seem to mind. They laughed and joked through the meal as if they were on a picnic.

Lockie joined in the fun and he felt a great sense of freedom. Eating at the Farrells was different – Mrs Farrell watched over them while they ate and she kept on reminding them about their table manners. The Wheelers stuffed bread into their mouths until their cheeks bulged and Lockie couldn't make out what they were saying. Their laughter was contagious, and he laughed with them without knowing exactly what they were laughing at. Little Tommy laughed so much that tears formed on his eyelids, and little pellets of half-chewed bread dropped from the corners of his mouth.

When they had eaten, Lockie went with Mickey along the road until they found a goat tethered to the fence. It was grazing the grass margin, oblivious of the stream of cars, lorries and huge articulated trucks that thundered by. Mickey began to milk the goat into a can he had brought with him. He jumped back and spilled a little of the milk when a loud scream cut through the roar of traffic. It was Rita Farrell.

'What do you think you're doing there?' she yelled at Lockie.

Lockie didn't answer – he didn't have an answer. He wasn't doing anything.

'Get home at once!' she ordered. 'Bad enough not to come home, but to be out tending goats with this – this –' She couldn't find a word bad enough for Mickey. 'This –' she went on, and finally settled for 'filthy thing' as the worst insult she could find.

'He's my friend,' Lockie said firmly.

'It takes one to know one,' she said.

That evening John Farrell was told the story by Rita, and she added little touches that made it sound a lot worse than it actually was. 'Left poor Gordon at home on his own … with a crowd of beggars out on the highway … tending tinkers' goats.'

John Farrell made Lockie kneel on the floor while he gave a stern warning: 'As long as you are one of this crew, don't ever – ever, I say – abandon ship like that again. That is desertion, and you could be keel-hauled for it.' His eyes were staring, and Lockie was looking straight up his nostrils as he stood over him. 'I'll have you put in irons if you do that again. Do you understand?'

'Yes,' Lockie said, trembling.

'That's not the way to answer me. What did I tell you?'

'Sorry!'

'I'll ask you again. Do you understand?'

'Aye-aye, Cap'n.'

'And there's something else. You're never again to have anything to do with that tinker boy. Rita will go to the school tomorrow to have you moved away from him in the class-room.'

But Mr Bradley didn't do as Rita Farrell asked. He and Mrs Farrell had a shouting match outside the classroom door. You could hear a feather fall in the room. All ears were straining, trying to catch what was being said outside. Only snatches of the conversation came through. They heard Rita Farrell say something about 'putting decent children beside tramps like that', and Mr Bradley could be heard shouting pompously, 'Nobody, but nobody, tells me how to organise my classroom!'

Mickey and Lockie were not separated, and Lockie apologised to Mickey for the insults Rita Farrell had thrown at him.

'It doesn't matter. We're used to that. Names never broke a bone yet,' Mickey said. He was only young, but he had an old saying to cover every situation.

'Anyway, I'm ashamed,' Lockie said.

'Why should you be? You had nothing to do with it.'

Their friendship stood firm in spite of everything, and Lockie was glad for it.

≈   ≈   ≈

A week later Mickey told Lockie that his father had been taken to the garda barracks for questioning the night before.

'What did he do?'

'Nothing.'

'Then why were they questioning him?'

Mickey wouldn't tell him. They walked around the playground and Lockie kept asking, but he got no answers. 'I thought we were friends,' he said.

'We are,' Mickey said, and Lockie could see that he wanted to tell him but something was holding him back.

'You're the first friend I ever had,' Lockie persisted.

'All right, then! I know it wasn't you who told them my da was trying to get you to come away with us, but someone did.'

Lockie stood still. He was shocked.

'Mickey,' he said, 'I never said that to anyone. Cross my heart and hope to die if I tell you a lie.'

'I know you didn't.'

'But who did?'

''Twas your father told the guards.'

'He's not my father, and he's a bloody liar. I'll go to the guards and tell them the truth.'

'Don't. It's all right. My father doesn't mind. Every time something happens, the guards call one of us in to ask us questions. We're used to it.'

'But we're still friends.'

''Course we are.'

〰 〰 〰

That evening, when John Farrell came home, he faced a mutiny in his ship. Lockie flew into one of those awful rages that got him into trouble. His face was flushed and he shouted at the top of his voice, 'Liar! Cheat!' and he kicked a cupboard door and banged the living-room table with his fist.

Rita Farrell knelt on the floor with the two smaller children, her arms around them as if to protect them from the raw fury that had erupted in her living-room.

John Farrell caught Lockie by his elbows and forced him, kicking and shouting up the stairs. He pushed him into the bedroom, slammed the door behind him, and locked him in.

'Nobody is safe with you in this house,' John Farrell shouted through the door. 'I'm warning you now, I'll get a pair of handcuffs tomorrow, and if you ever behave like that again I'll cuff you to the apple tree in the back yard and leave you there until you learn to control yourself. Is that clear?'

'Yes.'

'What?'

'Yes. If you want me to say "Aye-aye, Cap'n", you can forget it.'

Lockie heard his footsteps marching down the stairs.

≋   ≋   ≋

Mickey wasn't at school the next day. Lockie asked Mr Bradley where he was.

'Got word this morning, Lockie. His family has moved on. You were good friends, weren't you?'

'Yes, sir.'

'Too bad, but that's the way with Mickey's people. Here today and gone tomorrow.'

Mickey's departure was the last straw. Lockie decided there and then that he would not return to the Farrells after school. He knew what he would do. He had seen boats moored at the pier, and he would take one and row out to some island where he would be free of Farrells and Miss Cuneens and foster families and schools and cheats and liars forever.

CHAPTER FOUR

On the High Seas

When Lockie got into the small boat moored at the pier, he hadn't a clue where to go to find his island. But one thing he knew for sure – he wasn't going back. He cast off the mooring rope and fixed the oars in the oarlocks. He pulled away from the pier.

At first the boat turned clockwise in a circle, Lockie's right hand being stronger than the left. After a while, however, he got the hang of it and the boat moved slowly out to sea. Nobody on the pier seemed to notice him rowing away.

The day was calm and there was scarcely a ripple to hamper his progress. When he got tired, he took a rest. Then he rowed again. He was going away from Cloughlee and the Farrell household and that was okay. Eventually he was so far from shore that the pier and the seafront dropped out of sight below the horizon.

A wind blowing from the east chilled the air. The water became choppy, and the boat began to rock. Lockie lay down under the thwarts to shelter from the cold breeze.

It was pleasant lying there in the rocking boat, listening

to the slapping of the water against the timber hull. Lockie made no attempt to resume rowing. His troubles seemed far away as he lay on the bottom of the boat, out of the wind and the cold. If he never saw land again, he wouldn't mind. He fell into a sound sleep.

〰   〰   〰

When Lockie woke up, the boat was rolling and pitching ever so gently. He could hear the water lapping against its sides. At first he couldn't remember where he was.

He gripped the gunwale and sat up. He was cold and stiff, and raising his body made his muscles ache. He saw that he was alone, in a small boat about a hundred yards offshore, drifting slowly past a long golden strand, and then he remembered what had happened.

A few flat-bottomed clouds were catching fire from the sun setting beyond the hills that backed the strand. Maybe it wasn't a setting sun, but the dawn of a new day, and a search for him had already begun. No! It couldn't be a new day. The sun went down behind the land and rose out of the sea. Lockie was sure of that. So it must be evening. Night was coming.

Just then he noticed a moving speck at the far end of the beach. The speck grew larger as it advanced towards him along the water's edge. Soon Lockie saw that it was a man, paddling through the shallow wavelets. The man saw the boat and stood gazing at it.

Lockie crouched down and peeped over the gunwale. What was he going to do? He looked out to sea, it was endless and empty. The land was solid and inviting. It was either drift away to that vast desert of water or row ashore and take his chances. At the very worst, he would be sent back to the

Farrells. Was that worse than dying of starvation in a small boat far from land?

But where were the oars? He had forgotten to haul them in when he fell asleep. They must have slipped out of the oarlocks and drifted away. Now he was helpless. The boat was moving slowly away from the shore, so he had to make up his mind quickly.

Lockie stood up, put one foot on the gunwale, and jumped into the water. It was deep and swimming was difficult in his clothes. He managed to wriggle out of his jumper and force his shoes off. It was much farther to the shore than he had realised, so he grew tired and had to float on his back.

Once he almost lost consciousness, but sea-water ran into his open mouth and up his nose, making him cough and splutter, and it revived him.

Eventually, between swimming and floating, he made it to shore, but he was so exhausted when he got there that all he could do was flop down on the sand. He closed his eyes and lay there.

'What's this? What's this?' A sharp voice startled him. Lockie struggled up to a kneeling position.

'Wet! All wet!'

The owner of the voice was tall, bony and dark, with a thick stubble of speckled whisker. He bustled about the kneeling boy, jerking his head from side to side like a cat examining a toy mouse, not knowing whether to pounce or leave it alone.

'Get up,' he ordered. 'You can't stay lying in the water all night.' The stranger pecked the air like a bird as he shot out the words.

'Get up. Get up!' he said again.

'I can't,' Lockie whined. 'I'm exhausted.' Lockie's eyes filled up with tears, his lower lip quivered, and in spite of his best efforts, he began to cry.

'Who are you? Where were you coming from in that boat?' the man asked.

'I– I–' Lockie hesitated. 'I don't remember.'

'Aha-a-a!' the man shouted, as if he had made a brilliant discovery. 'Loss of memory!' and he continued soothingly, 'Poor little lad. Don't cry. It'll come back.'

Lockie was overwhelmed by the man's sympathy, and he cried even more copiously.

The man bent down and lifted the boy up in his arms. He carried him along the beach and over the sand dunes until they arrived at a wide hollow. The bottom of the hollow was littered with clothes, and at the side was a cart, the front shafts supported on two forked sticks which had been driven into the ground.

Halfway up the slope on the opposite side was an animal unlike any that Lockie had ever seen before. Was it a donkey, or a pony? The head and especially the ears were like a donkey's, only bigger. Its coat was not the shaggy coat of a donkey but smoother, like a pony's, and dark brown, almost black, in colour. The animal was tethered by a long rope to a thorn bush.

It looked up when Lockie and the man came into view over the top of the slope, but resumed grazing almost at once, reassured, no doubt, by the sight of its master.

'That's Rosie,' the man said.

Lockie was too tired to offer a comment.

'Come on, we must get you into dry things as quickly as possible,' said the man. 'We don't want you to catch a cold.'

He rummaged among the clothes and shoes littered on

the ground. He chose a few articles and threw them to Lockie.

'Take off your wet things and put those on,' he said.

By now Lockie felt strong enough to protest. 'They're miles too big for me,' he said indignantly as he examined the trousers, shirt, shoes, and jumper he had been given. 'Only the shoes fit.'

'It won't be for long, only until your own stuff is dry,' the man said. 'Put them on and sit down there. I'll be getting something to eat.'

When he heard the word 'eat', Lockie realised how hungry he was. He pulled off the wet clothes, and hurried into the large garments provided by the stranger. In the meantime the man bustled about the hollow, gathering dry sticks and grass for a fire.

'Come over to this end,' said the man when the fire was ablaze. 'The wind is east tonight.'

Lockie staggered in the outsize trousers through the scattered clothing to the other side of the fire. He lay back on a heap of old clothes. It was pleasant. The fire was warm and his resting place was comfortable.

CHAPTER FIVE

Under the Stars

'What's your name?' the man asked, and he continued at once, 'Oh, I forgot. You don't remember.'
Lockie remained silent.

'Don't worry, boy, you'll remember in time, but you must have a name. I can't call you if you don't have a name. Would you mind if I gave you a name?'

'What name?' Lockie asked doubtfully.

'Moses, ' said the man, grinning as if he had solved the riddle of the universe. 'I think that's a good name. Suitable too.'

'I don't like it,' said Lockie. He had always wanted to know who he really was. Having yet another name would make him feel even more of a nobody, as if any old name would do him.

'But it's the right name for you,' the man said. 'Do you know what "Moses" means? "Taken from the water." That's what it means. And isn't that what you were? Taken from the water.'

Lockie didn't answer. The man went to the cart and took out a camping stove. He lit the jets. He filled a billy can and a tin can with water from a large plastic container and set them to boil on the stove.

'But I've no name for you,' Lockie said. 'What will I call you?'

'Call me Dadge to rhyme with badge or cadge,' the man answered.

'That's a funny name.'

'Short for *Adagio*. Something to do with slow music. A young lad called me that one day. We had done near forty miles that day, and when we got to the village of Knocknamona in the County Kerry, poor old Rosie was ready to drop. The village street is on a steep hill, and the unfortunate animal was hardly able to put one foot in front of another, never mind pull the cart up the hill. If you saw us, you'd be hard put to know whether we were going forward or backwards or stopped entirely.'

Dadge went to the cart and took out a large canvas bag. From it he drew enamelled mugs and plates, spoons, a knife, and laid them on the ground before them.

Then he continued, 'I had to get down off the cart and walk at Rosie's head. A young lad came out of a house, a young lad carrying a fiddle case. He stood on the footpath and stared at us, and then he began to laugh – out loud. People came out and stood at their doors to watch us going by. The young lad pointed at me and shouted, "Look at him, *Adagio*!" The name stuck and later on it got shortened to "Dadge".'

Soon they were eating. Lockie was so hungry that it was as good as a feast. The slightly salted butter and brown bread were delicious. The tea was strong and sweet. He loved the smoky flavour of the tea and the picnic feel of the meal.

When they had finished, Dadge went over to the funny-looking donkey and stroked her neck. She tossed her head and continued browsing the grass. Dadge checked the rope which tethered her to the bush. He put some fresh wood on the fire and came and sat down.

'What kind of a horse is Rosie?' Lockie asked.

'Everyone knows that isn't a horse. It's a jennet.'

'What's a jennet?'

'A jennet is a kind of donkey.'

'What kind of a donkey?'

'A donkey with a pony for a father, if you know what I mean,' Dadge said.

Lockie said nothing, though he still wasn't quite sure what a jennet was.

'What are you doing out here with a jennet and cart?' he asked.

'That cart is my mobile home,' Dadge said, and he raised his eyebrows and threw a glance at Lockie. 'The jennet is my tractor for pulling the mobile home from one place to another.'

'That's crazy. You'd be killed by the big lorries flying along the road every day, and speed hogs in sports cars.'

'I don't go near the big roads,' said Dadge as he poked aimlessly with a stick at the red embers. 'When I have to go on a main road, I leave it all to Rosie. She's a wise old jennet. She knows how to stay in by the grass margin, and she takes no notice of the noise.'

'It's still a mad way to travel,' Lockie insisted. 'Why don't you get a van?'

'A van!' Dadge said, and Lockie could hear the contempt in his voice. 'Even if I could afford one, I wouldn't want it.'

'Why not?'

Dadge stopped poking the fire and looked at Lockie. 'Think for a minute, Moses,' he said. 'Suppose I had a van, would I get to see the countryside when I was flying by?'

'You might if you went slow enough.' Lockie was trying to divert Dadge from thinking about what should be done with himself.

'Slow or fast,' Dadge said, 'I'd have to watch the road in case a bigger fool than myself was coming against me.'

Lockie had run out of things to say, but he wanted to keep the debate going. He turned over and rested on his left elbow.

'I still think it's crazy,' he said.

'Why so?'

'It's too slow.'

'What's the hurry?' Dadge said dreamily as he gazed at the fire. 'Don't you know it's nicer to be going somewhere than getting there.'

Again Lockie was at a loss. He had no answer to that.

'Nobody goes around on a cart nowadays,' he said in one final, feeble effort to distract Dadge.

'You're wrong there, Moses. I do.'

'But no one else.'

A silence followed, and Lockie's main concern kept nagging at him. He decided to get it over with.

'What are you going to do?' he asked.

'How do you mean?'

'What are you going to do about me?'

Dadge thought for a while. 'I don't know yet. First I want to find out who you are. Then I can be thinking what I should do about you. But now it's getting late and we must sleep.'

Dadge stood up and looked at the sky.

'It's going to be a fine night,' he said, 'a light wind and clear skies. But it'll be cold before morning, and the dew will be heavy. We must be well wrapped up.'

He went to the cart and got a sleeping bag and several rolls of tarpaulin.

'That's yours,' he said, handing the sleeping bag to Lockie. 'Stretch it out there for yourself and get into it.'

When Lockie was in the bag, Dadge put a bundle of clothing under the flap to make a pillow. Then he took a few sticks from the heap of firewood and hammered them into the ground near the boy's head. A piece of tarpaulin laid over the sticks made a small cave-like shelter.

'How's that now?' he asked.

'Great,' Lockie answered.

He was cosy and warm in his sleeping bag. He was excited about sleeping in the open air for the first time in his life and forgot to worry about what was going to happen to him. His head was raised slightly on the 'pillow' and he could look out of his little cave at the sky. Already it was pierced by a single bright star.

Dadge was busy about the hollow, making his bed with sheets of tarpaulin and old clothes, stowing things away in the cart. Lockie heard him go up the slope and say a few soft words to the jennet. There was a hissing and crackling as Dadge dowsed the fire. Then Lockie could hear him settling into his own 'sleeping bag' a yard or two to his left.

The sky darkened slowly, and, as it did, more stars peeped through. One by one they came at first. Then they came in clusters, so fast that where one moment a patch of dark sky was opaque, an instant later it was peppered with pin-pricks of light. Soon the whole heaven had deepened to a dark navy and it was riddled with stars.

'Pins and needles,' Lockie said aloud. Talking to himself at night was a habit he had developed over the years.

'What's that?' Dadge asked.

'I was just thinking. The sky looks like it has pins and needles.'

'It does too, boy. It does. Stop thinking now, and go to sleep.'

Lockie closed his eyes, and his ears and mind began to adapt to a new set of night sounds. There was almost a total quiet apart from the hush and muffled drumming of the sea as the waves collapsed gently on the shore.

'Dadge,' he called.

'What is it?'

'About tomorrow …'

'Tomorrow is tomorrow. We can do nothing about tomorrow until it comes. Now go to sleep.'

Later a piercing cry brought Lockie half-awake.

'What's that?'

'A curlew.'

He half-opened his eyes and saw the sky still filled with stars. He felt reassured and dropped back into a deep, sound sleep.

CHAPTER SIX

On the Road to Coonmore

The sting of smoke in his nostrils woke Lockie. He raised his head and saw the sky, a bright blue semicircle at the mouth of his shelter. Dadge was bending over the camping stove, arranging his cooking tins on the jets of blue flame.

'Ah, you're awake,' he said when he saw Lockie sit up and look around him. 'Good morning to you, Moses. A beautiful day and a shame to be in bed.'

'What time is it?' Lockie asked. The time didn't matter really, but he wanted to say something, and he was afraid to talk about what was really on his mind.

'It's early,' Dadge answered. 'The sun is not long up. The nicest time of the day.'

Lockie got up. The hollow had been cleared of all the debris that littered it before he went to bed. There was only his own sleeping gear. His clothes were dry and he put them on. After breakfast they stowed the rest of the gear on the cart.

'What are we going to do now?' Lockie asked.

'First of all we're going to Coonmore to see a man, and then we might go to the garda station.'

'The garda station?'

'Yes.'

'What for?'

'How do you think we can find out who you are and where you came from? The guards are the lads who can find out about things.'

Lockie was silent for a while. Then he asked, 'How will they find out who I am?'

'They'll send out word, of course,' said Dadge.

'How?'

'Don't you know? The papers, the radio. Television too. A photo of you on the screen, and the news woman saying,' and Dadge made an effort to imitate the voice of the news-caster. 'Does anybody know this boy? He was found lying on the shore at Kiltarrant Strand, at the water's edge. If anyone has seen this boy, would they please get in touch with the gardaí at Coonmore.'

Dadge was observing Lockie closely as he spoke. But Lockie didn't notice. He wasn't too happy at the thought of the guards finding out who he was. Maybe he could run away before that happened.

Dadge stood up and poured hot water from the billy can over the plates and cups they had used. Then he stowed all the food and crockery in the canvas bag and placed it in the cart.

Lockie watched as Dadge took the harness from under the cart. He took all the bits and pieces and brought them to the jennet. 'What's that?' Lockie asked him.

'A bridle.'

'What's it for?'

'Moses, boy, you don't know anything about anything. A bridle is part of the tackle. It carries the reins, and the bit.'

One by one he took the pieces of the harness and dressed the jennet. He showed each item to Lockie as he took it and put it on the jennet: 'This is the collar and that's the hames.' He named everything – the straddle, the girth, the britchin and the breastplate. Finally he raised the shafts of the cart and backed the animal between them.

'These are the traces. I'll hook them to the rings in the hames and we'll be ready for the road.'

When the jennet was tackled, Dadge climbed up on the cart, and sat on the seat.

'Climb up here beside me,' he said.

Lockie jumped on.

The cart wagged from side to side with the movement of the jennet. The jennet looked peculiar from Lockie's position, a ridged back sloping down on each side towards the shafts, and zig-zagging as the four legs moved in sequence, like a giant earwig wriggling along.

The jennet laboured up the sloping side of the hollow and went at a walk through the field beyond. They crossed the field, passed through an opening in the fence, and came out on a narrow road.

Lockie watched Dadge manage the jennet. He made a clicking sound of encouragement occasionally and raised the reins and let them fall lightly on the animal's back – more a pat of encouragement than a spur.

When they reached the road, Dadge pulled on the right rein and the animal turned right. He beat the reins on the jennet's back a few times and called out, 'Hup there now, Rosie my girl. Let's get to blazes outa here!'

Rosie broke into a trot and the cart shafts bounced up and down. Lockie thought it wasn't a very comfortable way of travelling.

They were passing through low-lying country, which rose and fell gently. The road was lined with whitethorn bushes, uncontrolled, so that in places they were as tall as trees. Gaps between them on the right revealed a calm sea, topped by a blue sky and some cauliflower clouds. To the left fields, hedgerows and trees stretched away for miles to a dim backdrop of low hills.

Dadge shouted 'Whoa there, Rosie!' The cart came to a halt, and Dadge raised his nose to sniff the air.

'Smell that now, Moses,' he said.

Lockie sniffed. He caught a faint scent of cut grass mixed with summer blossom and the salty tang of the sea.

'Do you smell it?' Dadge asked eagerly, his face intent.

'I do,' Lockie answered, but he wasn't quite sure what it was he should smell.

'Isn't it good to be out on a day like this, and free, and going someplace?' Dadge said, as he sat back on the seat and shook the reins to put Rosie in motion again.

〰 〰 〰

They met heavy traffic when they drove into Coonmore some hours later. At the bottom of the hill where the main road took a sharp left turn and a narrower road went straight on, Dadge took the narrow road away from all the traffic.

The houses in this part of the town were smaller. They drove round a corner and into a little *cul-de-sac* of about ten small, one-storey houses, five on each side, all identical. Each had one door and one window. The interiors were hidden from the view of people on the street by lace curtains hanging inside wide window sills. On the window sill of every house, as if by general agreement, stood a flower-pot containing a geranium.

The house at the end stood out from the others because it had been newly and flamboyantly painted – the walls a brilliant yellow and the door a glossy, gleaming red. Here they stopped. Dadge tied the reins to a lamp post nearby and went to the door and knocked.

CHAPTER SEVEN

New Friends

The red door opened just a few inches, and someone peeped out. Then a rich, female voice cried, 'Dadge!' and the door opened wide.

An old lady stood in the doorway. She was the size of a ten-year-old child. Lockie couldn't decide whether she was a dwarf or just a very small woman. She was smiling broadly at them.

Her thin hands waved and gesticulated, fluttering like a moth near a flame. She uttered little cries of delight as she fussed around Dadge.

Then, as if she regretted being so affable, her face took on a sullen look. 'I suppose you want to come in and rest your old bones,' she said brusquely. 'Come on in so.'

'Who's there?' came a man's deep voice from within. 'Who is it, Mammy Tallon?'

'It's that old tramp, Dadge, Pasha, and he has a little friend with him.'

Her grey eyes softened as she turned them on Lockie. 'A little friend with a sad face,' she added as she bustled ahead of the pair into the house.

'Come on in, Dadge,' the man said cheerily. 'And bring your young friend.'

The room was small, with a few chairs, a table, a dresser filled with gleaming ware, and a fireplace. It was too warm for a fire, so they had put a large vase containing sprigs of laurel in the fireplace. On a chair by the fire sat the man called Pasha. His face was brown from the sun, and deep lines ran down each side of a strong mouth.

Dadge and Lockie sat down side by side in two chairs opposite the man. The woman was busy about a gas cooker at the far end of the kitchen, removing lids from saucepans and looking at the contents, pouring water into the kettle, changing pots and pans from one position to another.

All the time she kept up a sarcastic commentary on Dadge's arrival. 'Now look at what the wind brought in, Pasha, the wandering beggarman, Dadge Mulcair, and his little friend. And didn't they time it well? Don't we know Dadge of old? He'd smell a bit of grub cooking from the other side of the hill.'

'There's no harm in that, Mammy Tallon. Haven't we enough for all?' the man replied.

'And that old crossbreed, Rosie, brought them over the roads to us.'

'Rosie's a good friend, Mammy Tallon.'

She and Pasha continued like this for some time as if Dadge and Lockie weren't in the room. To Lockie it sounded as if they didn't want himself or Dadge there. But Dadge didn't seem worried. Once, when the woman carried some cutlery to the table she put her toe under Dadge's outstretched feet and kicked his legs aside.

'Move them out of my way!' she said, and Dadge bent his knees and raised his feet as if the ground was on fire. Lockie was almost certain that she winked at him as she passed by.

'And you have a story for us, Dadge,' she said. 'Who is your sad friend?'

'I found him in the sea,' Dadge said.

Mammy Tallon stood still and raised an eyebrow. Pasha sat impassive, showing no surprise. Then Dadge told the story of finding Lockie, with the other man throwing in a question now and then.

'So here we are,' Dadge said finally. 'All I have to do now is go to the guards to see if they can find out who he is.'

All three of them looked at Lockie. He hung his head and remained silent.

'To the guards I must go,' Dadge repeated, still looking at Lockie. 'There might be a reward for finding him, that is if we could find out who he is.' He paused. 'If his memory came back.'

Lockie still didn't speak.

Mammy Tallon broke the silence. 'Look at me, boy,' she said. 'I won't call you "Moses". That's not your name, is it?'

Lockie didn't answer.

Pasha intervened. 'Tell us about yourself. Maybe we can help. Who are you?' He leaned forward, his dark eyes fixed on Lockie. Pasha had a way of looking at people, his eyes unwavering, as if he were totally engrossed in what they were saying. The boy sighed. He felt that those eyes were seeing into the centre of his mind.

'Lockie,' he said weakly.

'Lockie what?'

'Farrell. But Farrell is not my real name.' And he told them all about himself, about the Farrells and the Malones and the Cagneys and how they treated him.

While he was telling the story, Lockie noticed that

45

Pasha's cheeks tightened, as his own did, when he clenched his teeth.

They sat listening to him without comment, and he felt easy with them. It was as if his tongue loosened and all he could recall came tumbling out, the story of his life, from his earliest memories to the present moment.

There was no hint of self-pity in the telling. Once the old lady walked behind his chair. She reached out and laid her hand on his shoulder and squeezed.

'Do you remember anything from the days before you went to live in your first foster home?' she asked.

'Bits of things.'

'What things?' Pasha asked. 'Do you remember people?'

'Not really. I was very young.'

There was a brief silence.

'What else do you remember?' Pasha asked.

'Not much else. Just the families I was with.'

'Why didn't you stay with them?' Mammy Tallon asked.

'Always I did something and they got rid of me.' Lockie paused for a moment. 'I have a black temper,' he added meekly.

'Good!' Mammy Tallon said. 'I like a young fellow with a bit of spunk.'

They were quiet for a minute or two. Dadge looked at Pasha.

'We can't send him back,' Pasha said.

'Well then, what do we do?' Dadge said peevishly. 'We can't go finding another place for him to stay. Isn't that the guards job?'

'They'll send him back to the Farrells,' Mammy Tallon said.

'That mightn't be so bad.'

Mammy Tallon took some time to speak. 'All right for us to say that, Dadge. We've been living on the edge all our lives. We're used to no one wanting us.'

'I know,' said Dadge. 'I must be the most unwanted man in Ireland. I've been told to move on a thousand and one times. But what has that got to do with it? The guards are the best people to look after this young fellow.'

'The guards have to go by the rules,' Mammy Tallon said, 'but the rules don't always give the best answer.'

'You don't expect me to look after him, do you?' Dadge said indignantly. 'There's no reward for him. That's one thing for sure. And we have nothing to gain by holding on to him.'

'We can't send him back to the Farrells,' said Mammy Tallon.

'Who's we?'

'You, me and Pasha.'

'Well, speak for yourself, Mammy Tallon,' replied Dadge. 'I wouldn't have any trouble sending him back to the Farrells, but I'm not bringing him there. I have to go south, and I'm behind time already. I say let the guards handle it.'

'I'm not going back,' Lockie shouted. It was almost a scream.

'Ho–ho!' Mammy Tallon laughed, and she smiled at Lockie. 'Is that your black temper showing? Go on, boy. Have another shout or two. Shouting is great for cooling the nerves.'

Lockie's fury vanished and he was ashamed. 'Sorry,' he said.

The others stopped and looked at him, but he didn't dare to meet their gaze. He didn't want to see the rejection in their eyes. Then Pasha looked at Mammy Tallon. Whatever he saw in her gaze made up his mind.

'We must go south with him until we decide what to do,' Pasha said, and Lockie sighed with relief.

He noticed that Pasha said little, and it was difficult to tell what he was thinking from his face. His expression hardly changed. But Lockie sensed the quiet strength of the man, and though he didn't quite know why, felt safe in his presence.

'Who's we?' Dadge asked again.

'All of us.'

'Not me.'

'What's wrong with you, Dadge?' Mammy Tallon said. 'You know we can't let them have him back.'

'Too big a load for Rosie,' he said.

'We have our own transport,' Pasha reassured him.

Dadge laughed. 'Is it still able to go?'

'Better than ever.'

'Where in the south will we go?'

Pasha didn't answer him directly. Instead he turned to Mammy Tallon. 'I think it's time to pay a visit to your old home on Tallon Island. We haven't been there in a whole year.'

'About time you thought of it, Pasha. The house would fall to ruin if it was depending on you to look after it.' She said to Lockie, 'That's a lazy man there, Lockie. I hope you don't turn out like him.'

Mammy Tallon turned to Dadge. 'Will you come with us?' she asked.

'I haven't much of a choice, have I?' said Dadge and he pointed at Pasha. 'He has his mind made up and he always gets his own way in the end.' He paused for a moment. 'Ah, I'm only talking to be saying something. In my heart I don't want to see this young fellow going back to what he ran away from. Wasn't it I found him on Kiltarrant Strand?'

'Why can't we just stay here?' Lockie asked.

'Too many people,' Mammy Tallon said. 'And people near the big city wouldn't give a fivepenny bit for you. If one of them found you, they'd hand you over straight away.'

'But would I be safe in your house?' Lockie asked her.

'Safe as could be. My house is on Tallon Island, and the people there are my people. They wouldn't give the game away on you.' She smiled at him again. 'Would that be all right with you?' she said.

'Yes,' Lockie said.

'Come on then,' Mammy Tallon said, putting plates of steaming food on the table. 'Do you want me to eat it for you as well as cook it?'

They pulled chairs up to the table and tucked in to bacon, cabbage and floury potatoes. Lockie ate ravenously. The morning drive had put a sharp edge on his appetite.

He couldn't believe that they would help him to stay away from the Farrells. Never before had he met someone who was on his side. Maybe Miss Cuneen, but no one else.

'Why are you doing this for me?' he asked.

'Why not?' Mammy Tallon said.

'But you don't know me. You're all strangers.'

'You're hard done by,' Pasha said. 'Isn't that enough?'

'And why should they be the ones to decide what's best for you?' Mammy Tallon said.

'Who?'

'*Them*. The ones who run things. The ones who try to run our lives.'

CHAPTER EIGHT

The Journey Begins

When the meal was over, Dadge and Lockie went out to the cart while Pasha and Mammy Tallon prepared for the journey.

Dadge rummaged among the clothing in the cart and pulled out a small bag and an enamel pan. He spilled some oats from the bag into the pan and went to the jennet's head. He held the pan to her mouth and she munched the oats.

Lockie sat on the cart seat and Dadge leaned against the shaft while they waited for Pasha and Mammy Tallon. Lockie did not trust Dadge.

'You were going to dump me,' he said accusingly.

'Well, I changed my mind, didn't I?' Dadge answered.

Pasha and Mammy Tallon came out of the house just then. Lockie had to suppress a laugh when he saw Mammy Tallon. She was wearing dark trousers, a heavy jacket made from sheepskin, and a tight-fitting leather helmet. A pair of goggles rested on the front of the helmet just above her forehead. She was like a dwarf version of a First World War pilot.

Pasha was dressed in exactly the same style, but his jacket

was an old one of battered leather, and instead of a helmet he had a cloth cap. He wore faded leather gauntlets.

He disappeared into the lane running behind the house and emerged wheeling a motorcycle with side-car. The handlebars were enormous, like reindeer antlers. It was an ancient model, and there was something upright and sedate about the bike's design, as if it had been built for style rather than speed.

Dadge didn't seem surprised. He untied the jennet and sat on the seat. Rosie was anxious to move off, but Dadge held her back as he waited for Pasha to lock up. Pasha sat on the saddle of the bike and Mammy Tallon climbed on the pillion. Pasha took a map from the inside pocket of his jacket and opened it on the petrol tank in front of him.

'We'd best go the back roads,' he said. 'Too much traffic on the main roads, and anyway there might be a search out for this little fellow.' He cocked a thumb at Lockie. 'Dadge, you know the way. We'll go ahead. If there's anything suspicious – we can double back and warn you.'

They decided to meet at a quarry on the far side of the Ardilaun Gap and set up camp there. Pasha studied his map for a minute. Then he folded it and put it back in his pocket.

'Okay,' he said. 'We'll wait for you at the quarry.'

He stood up and kick-started the bike. It took three kicks before it burst into life. A short puff of smoke shot back from the exhaust. Pasha sat down and turned the throttle, and the noises of the engine increased. It was not the rough, loud rattle you might expect from such an old model, more a gentle purring as the engine ticked over.

He turned the throttle up still further, put his foot on the step, and the bike moved smoothly down the street and out of the *cul-de-sac* with Pasha and Mammy Tallon sitting up straight, like visiting dignitaries in a ceremonial parade.

When they had passed out of sight around the corner, Dadge shook the reins and said, 'Hup there now, Rosie my girl. Let's get to blazes outa here!' Rosie raised her head and ambled down the road, heading for the main street again. People on the footpaths stopped and stared. A few shouted greetings, 'Good on you there!' or 'Go on, mule!'

Dadge ignored them. He headed for the top of the town. There he turned off the main road and went down a narrower road, signposted to Coolderry. Rosie slowed to a leisurely pace, and Dadge didn't press her.

Dadge pulled into a farmyard and went to the door. He asked for a sup of milk, and the lady brought him a large bottle full of milk. She also gave him a square of homemade bread and a bundle of clothing.

Dadge threw the clothing into the cart. He searched for the food bag and put the bottle and the bread safely inside, then returned the bag to its place under the clothes.

'Out of the sun,' he explained to Lockie. 'Milk goes sour if it's a long time in the sun.'

'Did that woman know you?' Lockie asked.

'She should,' Dadge answered. 'I call there every time I pass. She's always good for a bite of grub and a clout or two.'

'What's a clout? I thought it was a wallop.'

'It is,' Dadge told him, 'but it's a piece of clothes too. "Cast not a clout till May be out", is an old saying.'

'What does that mean?'

'It means that if you take off some of your winter clothes in the month of May, you might catch a cold. Will you go easy on the questions now for a while. I need a bit of thinking space.'

They drove along in silence, and, in the afternoon, they

went through Ardilaun Gap, out of the shadow and into the sunny side of the hill. Dadge stopped the cart for a while and he gazed at a line of grey cloud just above the horizon to the west.

'It might make a dirty night,' he muttered almost to himself.

A few miles beyond the gap they came to the quarry. They went in through a wide gap in the roadside fence and rounded a few large mounds of gravel and broken stone until they were beside the cliff that was the inner wall. It was a huge quarry.

The old motor-bike was standing behind a clump of trees, and a brown, faded tent was pitched nearby. It had not been visible from the road. Dadge drove the jennet on and pulled up beside the tent.

'Pasha!' he shouted at the top of his voice. Just at that moment Pasha and Mammy Tallon appeared through an opening in a few sally trees at the side of the quarry. They were laden with brushwood collected in the wood further down the road.

'You got here,' was Pasha's greeting.

'Had a nice drive, Lockie?' Mammy Tallon asked Lockie.

'Yeah, it was wild – great.'

Lockie looked around, examining the camping site. It was ideal. The large mounds of gravel cut them off completely from the road. The only hint of the nearness of civilisation was the occasional hum of a passing vehicle.

'I didn't like the look of it out beyond the Blackstairs,' Dadge said. 'I think we must batten down the hatches tonight.'

'Aye-aye, Cap'n!' Pasha said, and they looked at Lockie and laughed.

The tent was pitched on a sloping, grassy sward, and Pasha began to dig a trench around it with a short spade he took from the side-car. In the meantime Dadge had untackled Rosie and tethered her to a tree away from the tent. There was a patch of grass there and she began to graze contentedly.

Dadge built a two-tier shelter, the body of the cart making the upper storey and a scatter of clothing on the ground the 'downstairs bedroom'. With a sheet of tarpaulin over the whole structure, it looked like a covered wagon in a wild-west film.

'Now,' Dadge said as he stood back and admired his handiwork, 'the rain won't bother us too much. Climb up there, Lockie, and see what it's like upstairs.'

Lockie climbed up to the bed on the cart and lay down on the clothing.

'It's okay,' he said. 'No, it's great.'

'Get the spade when Pasha is finished,' Dadge told him, 'and dig a trench around our tent. It doesn't have to be too deep, just enough to let the rain run off. Then cut a little trench from it down the slope to take the water away.'

'It's not raining.'

'Not now, but it's going to be one hell of a night of rain. Wait, you'll see.'

He and Pasha took plastic containers and set off to find drinking water. Mammy Tallon went into her tent. The flaps were pulled back, and Lockie could see her moving about on her knees within, getting it ready for the night.

〰   〰   〰

They ate at leisure, seated on large flat stones beside the campfire. When they had eaten, they sat gazing into the fire.

They talked in short bursts between long silences.

'How far is it to Tallon Island?' Lockie asked.

'About a hundred and eighty miles by road to Barrymore village,' Pasha told him, 'and the island is about two miles off shore.'

'Is it nice on the island?' Lockie asked.

'Tallon Island is the most beautiful place in the world,' Mammy Tallon said with pride in her voice.

'Why has it the same name as you?' Lockie asked her.

Mammy Tallon laughed. 'Oh, Pasha gave me that name. First of all it was just his name for me, but now everyone calls me by it –'

Pasha interrupted, 'I call her that because that was where I first set eyes on her.'

'But why do you call her "Mammy"?' Lockie persisted.

It took Pasha a long time to answer. He sat looking into the fire. 'Maybe a bit of wishful thinking,' he said eventually, so softly Lockie could hardly hear him.

Dadge jumped up, went to the pile of wood and threw a few branches on the fire. The flames shot up, lighting up the trees and the quarry walls. Lockie caught a glimpse of two bright eyes gleaming in the dark shade deep among the trees.

'Look, look!' he said excitedly, but suddenly the gleaming sparks were gone, and when Dadge and the others looked around, there was nothing to be seen but the flicker of firelight on the pale trunks of the trees.

'What was it?' Dadge asked.

'Eyes. I saw eyes, just there. Something watching us,' Lockie said, pointing to the spot.

'A rabbit, maybe, or a cat,' Dadge said. 'More likely a cat. Rabbits don't leave the burrows at night if there's anything around.'

'Could have been a fox,' Pasha said.

They were silent again, gazing into the curling flames.

'Time to hit the sack,' Pasha said at last.

Lockie climbed into his bed on the cart, and Mammy Tallon went inside the tent. Dadge checked Rosie, and, when he had crawled into the bed on the ground beneath the cart, Pasha dowsed the fire.

'Good night, all,' he called as he went into the tent.

'Good night,' Dadge answered.

'Good night,' said Lockie. From inside the tent came the voice of Mammy Tallon. 'Good night,' she said. 'And if you keep your mouth shut, you won't snore!'

Lockie was too excited and too full of thoughts to sleep. He lay awake, listening. A dog barked in a distant farmyard. Now and again there was the hum of a passing car on the road, and once he heard footsteps and the murmur of conversation as some late passers-by went homewards on foot. But gradually sleep stole over him, and he sank into a deep forgetfulness.

Some time in the course of the night he was awakened from a dream by the sound of drums. It was the spatter of raindrops on the tarpaulin over his head. The others must have slept with their mouths open because he could hear them snoring above the drumming of the rain.

He listened for a while and then began to feel drowsy. The steady tattoo of the rain soothed him back to sleep.

CHAPTER NINE

Battle at the Hillside Bar and Lounge

By morning the rain had ceased. After breakfast, when the tents and gear had been stowed away on the cart and the side car, Mammy Tallon and Pasha left on the bike. Dadge and Lockie followed in the cart. Their meeting place was to be a grove of pine trees just on the Monksville side of Bunbeg.

In the early afternoon Lockie and Dadge arrived at Ballysteen, a tiny hamlet of five or six buildings scattered along two hundred yards of road. There was a post office combined with a shop, a small two-roomed schoolhouse, a pebble-dashed grey house, and a church.

Beyond the church was a low, slated house, that looked like an ordinary house, except for the large board over the window which proclaimed 'The Hillside Bar and Lounge' in capital letters.

Dadge tied the reins to a gate pillar outside and turned to Lockie.

'Come on in,' he said. 'But hold your tongue. There's a

whole lot of people in this world who want to know too much about everything.'

He pressed the bronze latch on the door, swung it open and stepped inside. Lockie followed. The contrast between the half-light of the interior and the brightness outside obscured everything for a moment.

Then, as Lockie moved forward, a glint on a brandy-bottle on a shelf at the back of the bar established a focal point, a key note to which all the colours and lights were related.

'Sit there,' Dadge muttered, gesturing towards the wooden seat just inside the door, and Lockie sat down obediently. The window was behind him, and he could turn and look out at the fields and hedgerows dropping away to the floor of the valley at the other side of the road.

A lady came through from a room behind the counter as if in response to some signal. Perhaps she had heard the clack of the latch as Dadge opened the door.

Lockie could see only the upper portion of this bar-woman. She had plump clear cheeks and soft round shoulders.

She paused to identify her customers, and then set up a raucous, high-pitched racket, like a parrot alarmed by a cat at the door of her cage. 'Ah, will you look at who's here,' she squawked, her fat face crinkled in rapturous smiles.

'You're welcome, Dadge, old friend. Where have you been? Come on, sit down, and tell us all the news,' and she continued, at the same high pitch, to ask questions and shower welcomes and blessings on Dadge. He accompanied her clamour with little goat-laughs and meaningless pooh-poohing gasps, as if he wanted to stem the tide of her good will.

Then she raised her voice to an even shriller note and

called, 'Henry! Henry! Come and see who's here.'

Henry, a colourless man, came in his shirt-sleeves into the bar.

'Ah, there you are, Dadge,' he said in a deep voice that was in striking contrast to the woman's tremolo. Lockie assumed that they were husband and wife.

'Give that man a drink there, Gertie,' he said to the woman. 'He must have come a long way, and he'll want to wet his throat if he's to give an account of himself. Where were you this time, Dadge?'

'Oh, the same old route, up the west to Galway, down again, across the south to Wexford, and then up the coast to Coonmore, and now I'm working south again inland.'

Gertie began to fill a glass from one of the taps behind the counter.

'Anything new?' Henry asked, and both he and Gertie looked with eager anticipation at Dadge.

'Well,' Dadge began, but he paused as Gertie placed a glass of amber liquid with an inch of froth on top before him on the counter. He took a swig from the glass, smacked his lips, and continued his story, 'I was in Wexford town on market day, and I strolled into the market yard. There I saw a curious thing.'

He paused and took a long draught of the drink.

'A man had a stall there. Vegetables I think it was – carrots mostly. You might know the man. They said he was from around here. A middle-aged man, pale-looking. Wearing a cap.'

'Yes, yes!' Gertie said urgently to hurry him past the inessential details.

'Well, up comes a dealer fellow. Threatening-looking he was. "I know you," said the dealer, bold like, as if he had some grudge against the stall man. "I never clapped eyes on you before in my life," says the stall man.'

On the story went, about a bloody fight in the market place in Wexford town. Dadge was a master story-teller, and the bar people hung on every word.

Lockie sat listening. He wondered if Dadge just made the story up to entertain the bar people and get himself a free drink. Soon he lost interest in the story and fell to thinking of his own dilemma. It was all right while there was something to be done or something new to look at, but when he got bored the worrying came back, about what he had done and where he was headed.

Dadge's voice rambled on with an occasional intervention from Henry or Gertie – 'You don't tell me!' or 'Wasn't he the blackguard!' or 'Served him right!'

Lockie sat unnoticed, in his cocoon of private reflection. It was pleasant in the dim light of the bar, with the array of coloured bottles on the shelves, each filled with its mysterious potion, and gleaming like rubies, emeralds, and amethyst in the half dark.

The door opened, and a burly, fair-haired man came in.

'Good day to you, Peter,' Henry greeted him.

Gertie was engrossed in Dadge's story, so she shouted to someone within, 'Sonny!'

Lockie jumped out of his daydream and said, 'Yes.'

Gertie looked at him in amazement. She had not seen him until that moment.

'Glory be to God, child, where did you come from?' she said.

'He's with me,' Dadge said abruptly before Lockie could speak. 'Lockie Mulhall. That's who he is. Lockie Mulhall is his name. He's one of the Mulhalls.'

Lockie could see that Dadge was agitated, and throwing out words without thinking as if he wanted to fill all the silence with the sound of his own voice.

'Where are you from, Lockie?' Peter, the newcomer, asked.

'He comes from Kilbore,' Dadge answered for Lockie. 'From Kilbore he comes. That's to say he really comes from near Kilbore. Not too far at all from Kilbore.'

Sonny came out from the back room and joined Henry and Gertie behind the counter. All three were silent, listening to the exchange between Peter Murtagh and the travelling man.

'What's he doing around here, then?' Peter asked Dadge, seeming to accept that Lockie could not answer for himself.

But the more Dadge tried to conceal the truth about Lockie the less convincing he sounded. In the end Peter turned to Lockie and asked him where he was going.

'I'm going to my uncle's for my holidays,' he said, terrified that the truth would be discovered.

Dadge smiled and looked at Peter, as if to say, 'There now. Didn't I tell you?'

'For a holiday,' he said aloud. 'Just for a few weeks on holidays to his uncle in Freshford.'

'But why is he travelling with you?' Peter asked. 'At your pace, 'twill take another two or three days to get to Freshford, and that young fellow will have to sleep rough at night.'

But now that a plausible reason had been given for Lockie's presence, Dadge began to sound confident.

'My good friend, Jim Mulhall, asked me to bring him,' he said in a ringing voice. The unquestionable truth of what he was saying was implied in the way he spoke.

'"Bring him with you," said my friend, Jim Mulhall,' he

rambled on. '"To my brother Paddy near Freshford in the County Kilkenny. Straight to Paddy's house. Let him see a bit of the country on the way," he said. "There's no rush," said he. "Nicer to see the countryside," said Jim to me, "than to be stuck inside an old bus or car. Everything gone by," said Jim, "so fast that it's gone before you can get a look at it."'

Dadge spoke of the fictitious Jim Mulhall and his brother, Paddy, in reverent, singing tones as if they were kings or heroes, and he and they walked a world beyond the ken of mortal men like Peter Murtagh.

Lockie sat there on the bench by the door, hoping that Dadge would finish and get out of the bar quickly. But Dadge was wound up by then, and he turned on Peter Murtagh.

'And as for camping out,' he continued aggressively, 'what would be wrong with that? Won't he have a snug bed and a shelter from the night and the dew or the rain or the wind or any damn thing that's likely to come?'

'I'm not saying he won't,' Peter said. 'But –'

'And isn't that a pile better than you're used to?' Dadge butted in, thrusting his face forward and staring at Peter with wild eyes. 'Sure everyone belonging to you got knacky, dodging drop-down from the thatched roof whenever it rained.'

'What are you saying, you – you –' Peter was lost for words. No insult was great enough to match the slur Dadge had cast on his ancestral home.

The big man advanced, like an enraged gorilla, on Dadge. Lockie had to stifle a scream of terror. Henry and Sonny raised the counter flap and came outside the bar. Before Peter could come to grips with Dadge, they caught his arms and held him back.

'Easy there now, men,' said Henry. 'Nothing is worth fighting about.'

Gertie had gone pale. 'If you two want to hammer each other,' she screamed at her shrillest, 'do it somewhere else. I don't want blood spilt in this bar.'

Dadge moved towards the door. 'All right,' he said, 'if it's a fight you want, come on out of the woman's bar. Out there in the road I'll give you all the fight you can handle.'

'Let me go, Henry,' Peter roared. 'We'll go out to the road. We won't upset your bar.'

Henry tried to calm the men but it was no use. Peter was determined to have a fight and Dadge seemed eager too.

Lockie feared for Dadge. He was so thin and frail-looking, his face seeming more pale against the dark stubble of his unshaven jaws. And if Dadge were injured badly, Lockie would become the responsibility of Gertie and Henry, and where would that lead? Straight back to the Farrells, no doubt.

As they trooped out of the bar on to the road, Lockie untied the reins and climbed on to the cart. Rosie shuffled her feet as if expecting the order to move, but Lockie held the reins stiff and she stood there, waiting.

'Come on, Dadge,' he said. 'Don't fight him. Come on. Let's go.'

'Back away from that barrel of lard, is it?' Dadge said. 'Never let it be said!'

Peter took off his coat and laid it on the fence at the side of the road. His shirt-sleeves were rolled up, and Lockie saw his arms, thick as a man's thigh.

Dadge didn't remove his jacket or his cap, but took up a boxer's stance, left foot forward, chin tucked in behind right fist, and left fist forward. Peter stood square, both clenched fists held slightly forward at the level of his lower ribs. Lockie saw his fists as large as turnips and he feared again for Dadge.

Henry and Gertie and their son stood in the road watching. A man coming out of the post office shouted to those inside, 'A fight! A fight!' People spilled out of the post office, a woman shopper came up the road to look, and the crowd of onlookers grew.

Dadge stood on his toes and began to hop in a circle around his adversary. He reminded Lockie of someone on a pogo stick. Peter just stuck out his right hand and his fist smacked against Dadge's chin. Dadge was moving so fast that the blow merely glanced off him, but his cap shot into the air and he fell backwards. The post office man hurried forward and helped him to his feet.

'Run away while you can still run,' he whispered to Dadge. 'That fellow is as strong as a bull. He'll kill you.'

But Dadge just shook him off and resumed his hopping. The contest was not as one-sided as Lockie had expected. Dadged moved like a wasp, zig-zagging around the burly farmer. Several times he dodged the wild lunges and flailing fists of his opponent, and hopped in closer to plant one or two sharp blows on the other's face.

Lockie began to feel better.

Then Dadge hopped forward and delivered three sharp blows to Peter's chin. The farmer's head snapped back three times in quick succession, and he seemed to be growing less sure of the outcome.

Henry, the barman, stepped forward between the combatants, and said, 'That's enough now. We'll have no more fighting today.'

'No, it's not enough,' Dadge said. 'He started at me inside in the pub. It's not over yet.'

'Go away, Jack,' Peter said. 'I want to kill the dirty tramp.'

'Come on now, Peter,' Henry said, 'don't take any notice of him. Sure we all know what he is. A man like you should be above taking any account of what the likes of him would say.'

Perhaps Dadge too had had enough. He picked up his cap and put it firmly on his head and walked to the cart. He jumped up beside Lockie on the seat and took the reins.

'So they know what I am,' he said indignantly as he turned towards Henry and Peter. 'And the barman knows what the likes of me would be likely to say. And like his seed and breed before him in the long line of hucksters he came out of, he'll side with his regular customers and throw a poor man of the roads to the dogs or the devil. Come on, Lockie. I don't like this place, and I won't be back.'

He shook the reins and shouted, 'Hup there now, Rosie my girl. Let's get to blazes outa here!'

Dadge slapped the reins on the jennet's back until she broke into a canter. When they had put about a mile between them and the bar, he relaxed and allowed the jennet to slow to her normal walking pace.

'Don't tell Pasha what happened back there,' Dadge said.

'Why not?' Lockie asked.

'Because he hates violence. I don't know any man that hates violence more than Pasha.'

'Why is that?'

'He was in the war.'

CHAPTER TEN

The News Breaks

It was early evening when Lockie and Dadge passed through Bunbeg and went along a byroad signposted to Monksville. About a mile from the town they came to an abandoned house surrounded by an overgrown garden.

Dadge got down from the cart and led Rosie through an opening where there had once been a gate. He went to the back of the house, untackled the jennet and tethered her by a long rope to a fence post. Again his choice of a camping place was perfect. They carried the sleeping-bag, tarpaulin, and clothing through a wicket gate at the back of the house and into a clump of pine trees.

'Tonight will be fine,' Dadge said.

They gathered wood for a fire, and took it into the derelict house. The old kitchen had a flagged floor and there was an open fireplace with bits of charred wood. They made the fire there. In a short time it was blazing, the smoke flowing freely up the chimney.

'Where's Pasha and Mammy Tallon?' Lockie asked.

'In Bunbeg, I suppose. Pasha might've got a job or something to make a few pounds.'

'What kind of a job?'

'How would I know what kind of a job he'd get! Pasha is one of those people who can turn their hand to anything.'

They ate supper and waited for Pasha and Mammy Tallon. When Dadge and Lockie had washed up and stowed away the supper things, they went out and gathered more wood to keep the fire going. Then they sat cross-legged on the floor, their backs resting against the wall opposite the fireplace.

Lockie looked at Dadge. The firelight was dancing on his face, except where his brows cast a deep shadow on his eyes. He was quiet, day-dreaming, in strong contrast with the man who fought the farmer at Kiltarrant earlier.

'Why did you fight that man today?' Lockie asked.

Dadge perked up, startled out of his reverie. 'Ah, he wanted to know too much. A little bit more and they'd have taken you off me and sent you back.'

Lockie was puzzled: 'Wasn't that what you really wanted?'

'True for you.' Dadge turned to look at him. 'I don't like to be caught up in other people's business.'

He reached over, took a few sticks from the pile, and threw them on the fire, sending a flock of sparks flying up the chimney.

'There was no need for you to be caught up in my business,' Lockie said. 'I can look after myself.'

Dadge's mouth twisted in what might pass for a smile, and he raised an eyebrow. 'Oh, I could see that, when I found you lying on Kiltarrant Strand,' he chuckled.

'That was different,' Lockie protested. 'I'd swum a mile then.'

'It doesn't matter now,' Dadge said, and he resumed his

day-dreaming look. 'Pasha decided we'd take care of you, and that's that!'

'Oh, yes, it was Pasha who decided,' Lockie chided. 'Do you do everything Pasha says?'

'Yes,' replied Dadge. He stood up and looked out the window. 'If Pasha asked me to jump off the Cliffs of Moher, I think I'd give it a lot of thought.'

'Was that why you went to see him before you decided what to do with me?'

'Yes.' He continued to peer into the deepening dark outside the window. 'They're a long time,' he mused. 'They should be here by now. What were you pestering me about? Oh, yes. You see, I didn't know who you were. You could be the son of the King of Spain for all I knew. There might have been a reward for finding you.'

'Now you know there isn't, so why don't you dump me?'

Dadge returned to his place on the floor. 'Can't you let it alone,' he said impatiently. 'Why must you have to get to the bottom of everything? Let it alone and don't be annoying me.'

〰 〰 〰

It was dark when they heard Pasha's bike droning over the hill and coming to a stop outside the house. He and Mammy Tallon had eaten in a café in Bunbeg where Pasha earned thirty pounds for repairing a cooking spit.

'You've made the news, Lockie,' Pasha said when they had settled down on the floor.

'Where? How?' Lockie asked excitedly.

Pasha reached into an inside pocket of his leather jacket and pulled out a folded newspaper. He held it close to his eyes and read it slowly by the light of the fire. Lockie leaned over his shoulder as he read, and this is what he saw.

MISSING

A twelve-year-old boy, Lockie Farrell, of 73 Latch-
ford Gardens, Cloughlee, has gone missing. He was
last seen at about three o'clock on Tuesday last on
the esplanade at Cloughlee. His parents reported
to the gardaí that he did not return from school
on that afternoon.

A boat taken from its moorings at Cloughlee that
same afternoon was found on Wednesday evening
drifting near Kiltarrant Strand. It is thought the
missing boy may have been involved.

Reports have also been received of a boy answering
Lockie's description travelling in the north Wexford region in the company of a well-known
vagrant known as Adagio Mulcair.

They are travelling on a cart drawn by a brown
jennet. Anyone with any information is asked to
contact the gardaí at Cloughlee.

Lockie was filled with foreboding. How would Dadge take
the news?

'Oh, my God!' Dadge exclaimed, 'I'm ruined. Ruined,
that's what I am. A kidnapper. They'll have me down for
kidnapping or worse. Now wasn't I right? I should've taken
him to the guards.'

'Calm down,' Pasha said quietly. 'We must think about
this. We've got to find a way of getting to Tallon Island
without being seen.'

'You're gone daft,' Dadge said to him. 'The nearest guards barracks is what I'm looking for.'

'If you go there, you'll almost certainly be arrested for kidnapping,' Pasha said, and he eyed Dadge as he spoke.

'Dadge, you old rat rustler,' Mammy Tallon said. 'You'd turn him in, wouldn't you? You'd like to see him back in that house.'

'No, I wouldn't,' Dadge moaned. 'But listen to the two of you! I landed up with a pair of maniacs.'

'Look,' said Pasha. 'Let's sleep on it. By morning we'll be thinking clearer and we can decide what has to be done.'

Dadge grew calmer. He offered the room to Pasha and Mammy Tallon.

'No,' Pasha said. 'You and Lockie stay here. We'll go to the room next door. It's dry.'

But Dadge wouldn't sleep indoors. 'There is nothing like a bed under the stars,' he said, 'at the centre of the whole wide world, nothing but space stretching for God knows how far, the cool night air on your cheeks. Nothing like it to blow away your troubles. See you in the morning.'

Lockie and Dadge went to their beds in the pine grove. They lay awake for a long time, not speaking, preoccupied by the reports in the paper. Lockie thought of running away again, but where could he go? If it weren't for Pasha and Mammy Tallon, he would have done so, because he was convinced that Dadge would have him sent back to the Farrells.

But he was certain that Pasha wouldn't betray him. And he couldn't understand why he trusted Mammy Tallon as much as he did. She was an irascible and sharp-tongued old lady, but he felt that she was on his side. Dadge was half-afraid of her, Lockie could see that. But even in her most stinging remarks, he thought he detected an undertone of humour. To himself she was all kindness.

It was a quiet night, but the light breeze made a whispering sound as it stirred the crown of pine leaves above their heads. Lockie thought it was remarkably like the sound of the sea on Kiltarrant Strand on the first night of his freedom. Slowly it lulled him to sleep.

Morning came and they all breakfasted together in the old house.

'Well, Pasha,' said Dadge, 'have you come up with anything?'

'One thing is certain,' Pasha said. 'You and the jennet will be spotted as soon as you hit the road. If Lockie is with you, he'll be sent back. I think he should come with me, and Mammy Tallon should travel with you.'

'What good would that do?' Dadge asked.

'That way if you're stopped, they'll think that someone made a mistake, that you haven't got a young boy with you at all.'

'I don't know if 'twould work. That fellow I boxed saw him all right. They'd ask me where the young fellow had gone.'

'You boxed someone?' Pasha asked in amazement.

'Ah, just a few feints and jabs, don't you know,' Dadge answered, and he stood up and did some shadow-boxing around the room. It was plain that he knew he had blundered. 'You see, this fellow was asking a lot of hard questions about Lockie here, and I had some words with him. I'd say he was the one that said he saw me with Lockie.'

Pasha looked straight ahead and the muscles of his face

clenched. Dadge squirmed, waiting for his anger to subside. Eventually Pasha spoke, slowly and calmly.

'I believe you're right, Dadge,' he said. 'They will ask you where the boy has gone. But, I'm sure you could deal with those questions okay.' He laughed, all sign of anger gone.

'How?'

'You could addle them with a stream of words that don't say anything. I've heard you in action,' Pasha said, still smiling.

In the end Dadge agreed to bring Mammy Tallon on the cart, and Lockie went with Pasha. They were to meet on the far side of Monksville.

〰 　 〰 　 〰

Lockie found it a little scary at first on the pillion behind Pasha. He gripped Pasha's leather jacket at the sides and hung on.

At a wide, right-handed turn Pasha shouted back over his shoulder, 'Lean over like me as we round the turn.' Lockie followed Pasha's example and leaned to the right as the bike rounded the corner. They straightened up as they came out of the curve.

It was exhilarating, vastly different to the cart. They were nearer the road for one thing, and it flew past at a rate that Lockie found alarming, although they were travelling at only thirty miles an hour most of the time. Lockie peeped over Pasha's shoulder to see what lay ahead. The wind caught him full in the face, and it was cold.

He ducked down to shelter behind the wide back before him, and had to be content with seeing the world in a blur as it sped by. After about twenty minutes Pasha slowed down. They were passing through the tiny village of Kiltarr.

As they emerged at the other side, Pasha slowed to a stop.

'What is it?' Lockie asked.

'Did you see it?' Pasha said.

'No,' said Lockie. 'What was it?'

'A funfair. Let's go back and take a look.'

Lockie wondered what interest a funfair could hold for a serious man like Pasha. They doubled back and stopped beside the gate. Pasha put one leg on the ground and sat in the saddle looking at the brightly coloured stalls and games of a small funfair.

'Hop down,' he said to Lockie. When they had dismounted, he raised the bike up on its stand.

'You stay here,' he instructed, and he walked into the small field. He went between booths and stalls, past the swings to two caravans which stood at the back near a lorry. Lockie could see him knock at the door of one of the caravans, and a voice spoke within. Lockie didn't hear what was said, but the voice must have invited Pasha to go in, because he opened the door and vanished inside.

Pasha was in the caravan for a long time. Lockie grew impatient and began to wander around the fair ground. He peeped into some of the huts and found various games of chance: roulette, coconut shy, roll-the-penny, pellet-gun range, lottery. As well as swings and dodgems there was a merry-go-round with hobby horses and carts for the small children.

One booth raised his curiosity more than all the others. In flamboyant letters blazoned across the multicoloured facade patrons were invited to 'Come and see the strong lady. Stronger than any two men. A hundred pounds to any man who can beat her in arm wrestling.'

Lockie pulled aside the curtain that closed the doorway

and went inside. It was like a tiny theatre. Three rows of chairs faced a stage that was bare except for a chair and table at the centre. Heavy dark-green curtains were gathered at the sides.

'Lockie!' He heard his name being called and ran out. Pasha and another man were standing near the bike, looking around and calling out his name.

'There you are,' Pasha said. 'I told you to stay near the bike. Never do that again.'

'Sorry,' Lockie apologised.

'This is Job Diggin,' Pasha introduced the other man. 'He's the owner of this funfair. Moll, the Strong Lady, is his wife. At the moment he's short-handed, so he is taking us on. He knows all about you.'

'Don't worry, young Lockie,' Job said. 'You'll be quite safe here.'

He was a big man, red-faced, fair-haired, his torso like a barrel. He wore light oil-stained trousers and a dark blue vest which showed his huge brawny arms and a blanket of hair on his chest. His pink skin covered with shiny fair hairs reminded Lockie of a pig.

'What about the others?' Lockie asked.

'They'll join us,' Pasha said. 'I'll leave the bike parked at the front and they'll see it.'

An hour later Dadge and Mammy Tallon arrived. 'I thought we were on our way to Tallon Island,' Dadge said peevishly.

'And so we are,' Pasha said. 'This funfair is working its way south. They have bookings in towns on the way over the next three months. If we stay with them, we end up in Skeheen in the first week in September. We can get to the island easily from there.'

CHAPTER ELEVEN

Thieves at the Funfair

Pasha became chief handyman to The Arcadian Amusement Arcade, the name adorning a banner at the entrance to the funfair. Lockie was his assistant, following him around while he was working, handing him hammer or saw or spanner, and fetching whatever was needed from a huge tool box attached to the rear of Job's caravan.

As they worked together, they talked. Pasha talked more than Lockie had heard him talk before.

Pasha told Lockie that his real name was John Underwood, but he got so used to 'Pasha' that he preferred to be called by the nickname. Years before he had gone to Turkey on board a tramp steamer that called at Coonmore, and some know-all gave him the name. 'Pasha,' he told Lockie, 'is the title of an officer in the Turkish army.'

'You never say much about that short fuse the woman talked about,' Pasha said to him one day.

'What woman?'

'You know, the woman from the Health Board. The woman that fixes you up with foster families. You told us she said you had a short fuse.'

'That's my bad temper.'

'Have you?'

'What?'

'A bad temper?'

'Sometimes.'

'I haven't seen it.'

'I've no reason to show it.'

'And what would it take to show it?'

Lockie told him about the times he shouted or kicked something in a fury and about the trouble it caused him.

'When people slag me is the worst,' he said. 'I feel the temper rising in my head, and then I could do anything. I put my fist through a window in the Cagney's.'

Pasha thought for a while. 'Listen to me,' he said. 'Before you do something foolish just think about it. When someone says something you don't like, just count to ten before you do anything.'

'Okay. I'll try.'

Dadge had the job of running the roulette game. At first Mammy Tallon had no special duties. She cooked for Pasha and Dadge and Lockie. Otherwise she just sat in the tent or walked around talking to the others as they worked. She went to the village sometimes, to the supermarket.

Lockie went with her on the pretext of helping her to carry the purchases back, but often they could fit in a small bag and she didn't really need help with them. As they walked along the road, she told Lockie all about Tallon Island. She questioned Lockie about his own life.

'Why did you have to leave the Cagney family in Marino?' she asked.

'That was the worst of all,' he said. 'I think they were ashamed of me, and when their friends came to the house,

I was sent upstairs. I ran away when they sent me to the kitchen one evening because my foster brother's friend was calling. That time I was caught in Athlahan and Miss Cuneen came and brought me to her own house for a few days until she found a new place for me.'

'Was no one kind to you?'

'I suppose Miss Cuneen was. Mammy Tallon, do you like me?'

'Stupid question. Why do you think I'm running across the country with you? Of course, I like you, and so does Pasha.'

'But what about Dadge?'

'Yes, Dadge does too. But Dadge is a loner. He finds it hard to get involved with people, but I know he likes you.'

〰 〰 〰

In the evening, when it was time to open the fair, Lockie went to one of the caravans, the one Job's son Zack and his young wife Katy lived in. Zack gave him magazines to read, but he was bored.

Katy came in. 'What were you doing?' she asked.

'Nothing,' said Lockie, 'Just sitting here looking out the window.'

'Mind you don't go poking around our things.'

Lockie was indignant. 'I'm not interested in your things.'

'That's what you say. All innocent and that "God help us" look on that ugly face of yours. I wouldn't trust the likes of you from here to the door.'

Lockie couldn't think of anything to say. He was dumbstruck. Up to then he had had very little to do with Katy. In fact she seemed to make a point of not talking to him.

She left the caravan with a final warning: 'Mind what I said. Keep your paws off our things.'

Lockie couldn't understand why she was hostile. Maybe she was resentful of the kindness shown to him by everyone else. There was little he could do about her – except avoid her as far as possible.

He was still pondering what she had said, trying to make sense of it when the power was switched on and strings of bright bulbs lit up all round the fair. There was no need for them in the early part of the evening, but they added to the carnival atmosphere.

Loud speakers over the dodgem tent blared out pop music. Four young men and three girls arrived to help with the running of the fair. The fair was fund-raising for a local football club and the helpers were members of it.

〰   〰   〰

About two weeks after Lockie and the others joined the fair, he sat in the caravan one evening, watching people coming in until there was a sizeable crowd sauntering from booth to booth. The funfair had its own special music: the hum of the generator, the whine and thump of the dodgem cars, the creaking of the swings, the rumble of the merry-go-round, and through it all, the talking and laughing of the happy crowd.

Lockie opened one of the windows to let in the sound. That way he felt he was part of the fun. Dadge's roulette stall was close by and he could hear his voice: 'Come on now, ladies and gentlemen. Tonight we're giving away money. That's what we're here for, to give you money and send you home happy. Place your bets. Even money the black, two to one the red. She's going to spin now. Put your money down.'

Pasha passed by the caravan several times. He was carrying an oil-can and some oil-stained rags. Mammy Tallon spent most of the evening at the Strong Lady's tent. Lockie thought the dark-haired Moll was the most man-like woman he had ever seen, with well-defined muscles on her arms and the light fuzz of black hair on her upper lip.

Zack, a dark, thin young man, supervised the dodgems. Business was good for him. There was a queue of people waiting for a turn. All the swings were in constant motion. One of the young men from the football club was in charge there while Katy ran the merry-go-round.

Job was MC at the Strong Lady's booth. He was dressed in black suit, white shirt and black bow tie. His kinky fair hair, which was untidy and dishevelled during the day, was sleeked down with hair oil, and he looked like a circus ringmaster as he bellowed:

'Come one, come all! See "Madame Sampsona" demonstrate her strength. She will lift a weight greater than any man; she will bend six-inch nails; she will beat any two men in tug-of-war. One hundred pounds for any man who can beat her at arm-wrestling.'

The evening wore on and it grew dark. As it did, the lights seemed to grow brighter. Lockie watched some of the people amble slowly out the gate, in ones and twos and threes, while others came to take their place.

People dawdled from stall to stall, playing at one stall, then moving on to the next. It was no wonder that two young men drew Lockie's attention. They didn't play at the stalls. They just stood in the centre of the fairground and looked around, taking everything in.

They were carefully dressed in suits and they wore collar and tie. Most of the other patrons wore T-shirts and jeans, or, as the night air grew colder, went to the cars parked along the roadside and put on jumpers.

The two young men in suits wandered towards the caravans at the back. They came to the window and looked in, holding their hands over their eyes to see behind the bright lights reflected in the windows. Lockie slipped unnoticed to the side and stood by the door until they had gone.

They had been there on the previous night too, and Lockie had noticed them then. It was strange that they should visit the fair on two nights and not take some part in the fun.

Towards midnight just a few stragglers remained, and Job announced over the loud-speakers that the evening's entertainment was about to end. Soon the site was deserted.

A few lights were left on as the workers locked up and retired to caravan and tent or went to cars parked on the road. Katy came to the caravan and said to Lockie, 'Be off with you. It's bed-time.'

As they were settling down for the night in the two-storey tent Lockie told Dadge about the curious strangers.

'Job has to know about that,' Dadge said, struggling out of his bed.

'What is it, lads?' Jack asked when he answered Dadge's knock.

'Lockie here has a bit of news for you,' said Dadge.

Job asked them into his caravan. The night's takings were arranged in neat piles on a table and, Ned, the football club secretary, was sitting there counting it and entering figures in a notebook. Moll was sitting on a seat by the front window. Lockie told them about the two men he had seen prowling around the caravans.

Job rubbed his chin. 'It's odd,' he said at length. 'Dadge,

call Pasha and Zack. Well done, young Lockie. It might be important, and then again it might not, but you were right to tell us about it.'

Zack came first, then Pasha. They were followed almost at once by Mammy Tallon and a few moments later by Katy.

'What's the boy wonder up to now?' she asked.

The others ignored her remark, but Mammy Tallon looked intently at her.

Job told them what Lockie had seen.

'What should we do, Pasha?' he asked

'I think Ned should go home by some roundabout way,' Pasha said, 'and the cash could be kept here. Tomorrow we could ask the guards to be on the look-out for those lads.'

'What about going in the car with Ned?' Dadge said, his eyes bright with devilment. 'We could give them a reception if they tried something.'

'I like Dadge's idea better,' said Moll and she laughed.

'What about you, Zack?' Job asked.

'I'd go along with Mam and Dadge.'

Job too was in favour of Dadge's plan. So, when they had counted the money and put it in a locked leather pouch, the warrior group piled into the car, Ned driving, Moll crouched in the front seat, Job, Dadge, and Jack keeping low, out of sight, in the back.

'You stay together here, all of you,' Moll said to the non-combatants. 'Turn on the radio, Katy. It'll pass the time until we get back.'

Katy twiddled the knobs until she found a late-night music station. The four sat there silent, listening to the music and the prattle of Benny Gurney, the DJ, between tunes. They waited fifteen minutes. Then thirty minutes dragged by.

'I'm taking a phone call,' the DJ broke in on their thoughts. 'It's from the parish priest of Cloughlee, Father Michael Shanahan.'

At the mention of Cloughlee Lockie raised his head. Mammy Tallon turned towards the radio, but Pasha sat without moving. If the name Cloughlee meant anything to him, he didn't show it.

'Hello there, Father Michael,' the DJ said genially.

'Good evening, em, Benny,' the priest's voice came through slightly distorted on the phone.

'I believe you have a request, Father.'

'I have, Benny, but it's not a request for – em – music. It's about a missing boy.'

Benny invited him to elaborate, and he told the listeners about Lockie and how he ran away from his foster parents. Katy kept looking at Lockie, and it was hard to know whether she was smiling or sneering.

'I believe you have a personal interest in the boy, Father Michael,' the DJ went on, and it was obvious that he had been briefed as to the questions he should ask.

'That's true,' the priest told the world. 'His foster mother is my niece, my sister's daughter, and she is a wonderful and devoted mother. It is beyond anyone's comprehension who knows Rita and John Farrell to understand why Loughlin – that's the boy's name – should choose to run away from such a happy home.'

Lockie and Mammy Tallon were speechless when the conversation ended and the music began to throb again. Pasha was looking at Katy.

'Why don't you like Lockie, Katy?' he asked quietly.

'Me, not like him?' she said, and she was clearly taken aback by Pasha's question. But she regained her composure and said: 'Well, what I don't like is the way he took over here. Everyone is falling over themselves, trying to be nice to him. You'd think he was a prince or something.' Then she smiled, 'But a runaway! Now there's something interesting.'

'What do you mean, "interesting"?' Mammy Tallon asked her, and there was an edge in her voice.

Before Katy could answer, they heard a car drive into the field. Its doors slammed and Job's voice said, 'Good night, men, and well done!'

'Thanks,' a strange voice answered. 'We'll call in the morning to take a statement.'

They all came into the caravan.

'Who was that?' Mammy Tallon asked.

'The guards,' Dadge answered for the others.

Job began to tell them what had happened. About a half-mile down the road to the village the pair had a car parked across the road. It was impossible to pass.

But Dadge was bursting to tell the story, and he interrupted. 'You should've seen it,' he said, and he stood in the only space available to him in the middle of the caravan, his eyes popping out of his head, his hands gesticulating wildly, and the words cascading from his mouth with excitement.

'Ned slowed down and came up to the parked car and stopped. "Now!" says Moll, and she jumps out of the car. She got a hold of one of the robbers and held on to him. She had one hand on the back of his neck and the other was catching him by the hair of his head, like you'd catch a rag doll.

'In the back we were in each other's way. By the time we got out, the second robber had skedaddled down the road towards the village, and cleared a gate, like a scalded kangaroo. Zack went after him into the field but he lost him in the dark.'

He paused then and told the remainder of the story more soberly.

'We brought the fellow Moll had captured to the barracks. There was no one at the barracks, so we went to Guard Mitchell's and knocked at the door. We had to go back with him to the barracks and he opened up and called a squad car in Kilkenny on the phone.

'The squad car with two guards came after about half an hour. They put the robber in the cell in the barracks and then they drove us back here. Guard Mitchell has to stay on guard in the barracks for the night and he's not a bit thankful to us. The other guards said they would come back in the morning to take statements.'

'Was anybody hurt?' Mammy Tallon asked.

'No,' Job said.

'Aren't you lucky?' she said derisively. 'Like overgrown children playing cops and robbers in the middle of the night.'

'But we weren't playing,' Dadge said innocently. 'It was the real thing, and we caught one of them.'

'A lot of good that would do you, Dadge Mulcair, if you were stretched on a hospital bed with your skull cracked open,' Mammy Tallon said, and she and Pasha stood up and left the caravan.

CHAPTER TWELVE

Katy Blows the Whistle

Lockie was awakened in the morning by voices outside the tent. He sat up and saw two guards leaning against the bonnet of a squad car, talking to Job and Pasha. Their car was parked just outside Dadge's makeshift tent. One of them had a notebook open and a pen at the ready. Dadge came out of his downstairs sleeping quarters and joined them at the car.

Lockie burrowed down under the clothes. He decided to stay there until they had gone. He was terrified in case one of them should look into the tent, see him there and begin to ask questions about him. Job was talking: 'They were nosing around the caravans earlier in the evening and we got suspicious of them. That's why we went in the car with Ned.'

'We had an idea they were up to no good,' Pasha said.

'Shifty-looking customers,' Dadge suggested, not wishing to be left out of the conversation.

Zack joined them at that stage. He was followed at once by Moll and Katy.

'We think we know who the one who escaped might be,' the older guard, Guard Tomelty, told them. 'If we could get a description of him, we could have him brought in for questioning.'

The younger guard, Guard Stone, stood with his pencil poised, but no one spoke. Then Dadge blurted out, 'It was too dark to get a good look at him. And he took off as soon as the back door of the car opened.'

'But if you spotted him while he was wandering around here earlier, you must have some idea of what he looked like,' Guard Tomelty said.

'We never saw him until we jumped out of Ned's car down the road,' Dadge said.

'But who saw him nosing around the caravans here?' Guard Tomelty persisted.

'That was young Lockie,' Katy volunteered. All the other heads turned suddenly in her direction, but she didn't seem to care that she had betrayed Lockie.

'Could we have a word with young Lockie?' Guard Tomelty asked.

For a moment there was an uncomfortable silence. Pasha went to the cart, pulled aside the tarpaulin, and said, 'Wake up, Lockie! Come on out.'

Lockie crawled to the edge of the cart and lowered himself to the ground.

'We hear that you saw the two strangers at the fair yesterday evening,' Guard Tomelty said.

'That's right, sir,' Lockie said.

'Good man. You're a sharp young man, I'd say. I'll bet you could describe them down to the ground.'

'I got a good look at them,' Lockie said enthusiastically, hoping the guards wouldn't identify him. 'One of them had kind of brown hair,' he said. 'He was taller than the other fellow.'

'We know about him. Did you get a look at the other fellow?'

'I did. He was foxy-haired and he had a bony face with freckles. I noticed his arms.'

'What about them?'

'They were very long. When he stood with his arms by his sides, his hands came down almost to his knees. I don't think I ever saw arms so long.'

'That's great, Lockie,' Guard Tomelty praised him. 'We know our man now. Thank you.'

Guard Stone closed his notebook and put it in the pocket of his tunic.

'You long with the funfair, Lockie?' he asked casually, showing only a mild interest.

'No, sir,' Lockie said.

'Have you been to sea lately?'

Lockie felt cold, though the day was warm. He knew at once that his flight had ended. He was silent for a moment, then he blurted out, 'I'm not going back. I don't care what they do with me. I'm not going back.'

'Now who said anything about going back?' Guard Stone said. He turned to Job.

'Thanks very much, Job,' he said.

Then he turned to Pasha. 'And thank you too, Pasha,' he said, 'and it would be a nice thing if that young lad were still here when Guard Mitchell calls some time later today. You know what I mean!'

'I know,' Pasha said with resignation.

When the guards had gone, Dadge turned fiercely on Katy. 'You have a big mouth on you, Katy Diggin!' he said. Katy turned without a word and walked back to her caravan.

'She wasn't thinking,' Zack said, making an excuse for her.

'I wouldn't be certain of that,' Pasha said.

'What are we going to do now?' Dadge asked when the guards had gone. He was walking up and down in front of the caravans. 'We can't let them take him and send him back to where he doesn't want to go. Would you like to be somewhere you don't want to be?' he asked Pasha.

'Sometimes we don't have a choice.'

'You've surely changed your tune, Dadge,' Mammy Tallon said. 'I thought you didn't want the responsibility of him.'

'And I don't,' Dadge said. 'But never will it be said that Paddy Mulcair let down a friend.'

'Who's Paddy Mulcair?' Lockie asked. He was sitting on the cart.

'Me,' said Dadge. 'Not ever could it be said that Paddy Mulcair let down a friend.'

'I'll run away again,' Lockie said. 'I won't stay there if they send me back.'

'Let's go for a stroll to the village,' Mammy Tallon said to Lockie. 'I must get a few things in the shop.'

They left the fairground and walked at an easy pace towards the village. They went into blue shadow between rows of trees, oaks and ash side by side, arched over the roadway.

'Lockie,' Mammy Tallon said.

He looked at her face changing from dark to light as she walked through the splashes of sunlight that came through gaps in the trees.

'Yes?'

'Lockie, Pasha and I have been thinking,' Mammy Tallon

began, and then she paused. Lockie waited for her to continue.

'We have no children.'

Again she paused, and Lockie remained silent. This time the pause was longer.

'Lockie,' she said eventually, 'what would you say to living with Pasha and me?'

'You mean for always?'

'Yes.'

Lockie did not hesitate. 'It'd be magic,' he said. 'Would Pasha teach me how to ride the bike?'

Mammy Tallon laughed. 'I imagine he would,' she said. 'On the island anyway. There's no traffic to worry about there.'

When they returned to the fairground, Dadge looked at Lockie and said, 'I don't know why you're looking so cheerful. You're going back to the Farrells as sure as the Lord made sour apples.'

He turned to Pasha. 'Will we make a run for it?' he asked.

'No,' Pasha said. 'We'd never get away with it. Better to wait and see what the guard says when we offer to keep Lockie and bring him up as our own.'

'You're going to offer to do what?' Dadge shouted, astonished.

'We'll try to adopt him.' Pasha looked at Lockie, and there was a ghost of a smile on his lips. 'If he wants to, that is.'

~~~   ~~~   ~~~

Lockie was sitting on the edge of the cart when Guard Mitchell arrived. He was a big, heavy man and he walked slowly.

'Anybody home?' he said loudly.

Job came out of the caravan and Pasha and Mammy Tallon came out of their tent. They had all been trying to catch up on the sleep they had lost the night before. Dadge was still sound asleep under the cart. He hadn't heard the guard.

Guard Mitchell looked at Lockie and said, 'I suppose that's the young man who ran away from home.'

Nobody spoke.

'Who's in charge of him now?' he asked.

'I am,' Pasha said.

'Where's the fellow with the jennet?'

'He's asleep. He was up most of the night.'

'So were we all,' the guard said peevishly. 'I'll have to get that young lad back to his people.'

'He doesn't have any people,' Pasha said.

'I'm told he was with some good people in the town of Cloughlee.'

'Depends on what you mean by "good",' Pasha said. 'They were so good to him that the last thing in the world he wants is to go back to them.'

At this point Dadge appeared, rubbing his eyes and squinting in the bright daylight.

'Hello, Guard Mitchell,' he said. 'On duty, I suppose.'

'I believe it was you who found the young boy,' the guard said to Dadge. 'Wasn't it a wonder that you didn't try to do something about getting him back to his home?'

'I was going to do that,' Dadge said.

'A funny way you had of doing it, carrying him around the countryside on a jennet and cart. We know all about that, and we know about your assault on a farmer in Ballysteen.'

Dadge began to walk up and down. 'That's a rotten lie,' he exclaimed. 'I never assaulted no one. That fellow was the assaulter. Minding my own business I was when he started at me. Not taking a bit of notice of him when he started asking me things, like a bloody policeman – oh! saving your presence, Guard Mitchell.'

'Never mind,' Guard Mitchell said. 'The man is not pressing charges. My job now is to get this young fellow back to his people.'

'I'm not going back!' Lockie shouted. 'I want to stay with Pasha and Mammy Tallon. I don't want to go back there.'

Mammy Tallon came out of the tent and joined the group.

'Tell him,' Lockie said to her. 'Tell him I'm going to live with you and Pasha.'

'Pasha and I want to adopt him,' Mammy Tallon said to the guard. 'He wasn't happy in the family he was with but we're sure he'll be okay with us.'

'I'm sorry, Mrs,' said Guard Mitchell. 'I have a lot of sympathy with what you're trying to do, but it isn't up to me. I'll have to get advice. I'll go away and I'll come back when I have news. In the meantime I must ask you not to leave the district until this thing is sorted out one way or another.'

Job had been standing there, listening. When the guard had gone, he said to Pasha, 'If they are trying to decide whether you're a suitable person to look after a child, they might want to know how you make a living. You can say you have a permanent job with the funfair.'

'Thank you, Job,' Mammy Tallon said. 'The thing is they might not like him to be with people who are always on the move. We must think about that.'

CHAPTER THIRTEEN

Back to Cloughlee

When Guard Mitchell returned later in the afternoon, he was not alone. With him were Father Shanahan, the parish priest of Cloughlee, and Miss Cuneen. All three arrived in Miss Cuneen's red Fiesta. Job and Moll had gone to Kilkenny for the afternoon and they had given the key of the caravan to Mammy Tallon.

'You can make a cup of tea for the guard,' Moll had said to her. 'It might soften his heart.'

'Here we go again, Lockie,' Miss Cuneen said. 'This time I am afraid you are in real trouble.'

Mammy Tallon invited them into the caravan where they sat on the bench seats at either side of the table. She busied herself near the gas cooker preparing tea, and Dadge tried to make conversation to fill the silence, as no one seemed anxious to broach the subject of Lockie.

'A fine day, thanks be to God,' he said.

'Powerful,' Guard Mitchell agreed.

'The corn is coming on nicely,' Dadge continued.

Their conversation went on to deal with the snow of January and the rain of the spring, the frost of the first week in May and the fine weather in July.

The priest, Father Shanahan, sat brooding, not saying a word. Lockie watched him anxiously, because he knew that priests had a big say in affairs.

This was a thick-set man, red-faced, greying hair. His most outstanding feature was a deep scar by his right nostril. It ran from just under his eye almost to his lips. Lockie thought he looked like an old viking warrior.

When they had been served the tea, Miss Cuneen spoke. Lockie had seen her in action a few times. She was always the first to speak.

'Here we are,' she said. 'I've come to look after Lockie again.' She smiled at him. 'By now we are old friends, isn't that so, Lockie?'

'Yes, Miss Cuneen,' Lockie said meekly.

'What kind of looking after now would you be talking about?' Dadge asked.

'Well, he can't be left here. We must see to it that he is properly cared for,' Miss Cuneen said, mouthing each word meticulously, and paying particular attention to final Ts and Ds.

'He is.' Pasha spoke for the first time.

Father Shanahan intervened: 'That may be a moot opinion.'

'What's this moot stuff?' Dadge asked belligerently. 'What has moot got to do with anything? Let me tell you this, Mr Priest, sir, that young fellow is not going back to the house he was in, moot or no moot!'

'I know the Farrell family well and I can assure you that they are excellent people, decent and most diligent in all their duties as parents and Christians.'

'But he doesn't want to go to them, so what do we do now?' Mammy Tallon asked.

'I am sorry to have to say this, but there is no prospect of placing him with another family. The Farrells are his only chance,' Miss Cuneen said.

'So what's going to happen to him?' Dadge asked.

Miss Cuneen hesitated before replying softly. 'If it's not the Farrells, I can't see any alternative to some institution.'

'He's not going to the Farrells,' Pasha said quietly. 'Nor is he going to any institution.'

'I don't understand, Mr – ah,' the priest hesitated.

'The man's name is Pasha,' Dadge intervened, 'and there isn't much to understand. He said the boy was not going to the Farrells or any place like it, and I say it too. For heaven's sake, I wouldn't let them in charge of my old jennet.'

The priest continued to address Pasha, as if Dadge hadn't spoken at all.

'I'm sorry, Mr Pasha. I can't understand your reluctance. The Farrells are an excellent couple, most conscientious, devoted to their children and caring, full of Christian concern for their welfare. And think of the humiliation they'd have to suffer if the child is removed from them without good reason. Their standing in the community and with the Eastern Health Board is damaged almost beyond repair–'

Dadge took to pacing up and down the tiny space between the table and the cooker, two steps one way, then two steps back. He began to fling out words again.

'Christian concern, is it?' he said. 'So it's Christian concern they have now, is it? So that's Christian for you. I know people like them. If that's Christian, then you can keep your ould Christian. Christian concern, ha-ha-ha.'

'Does he have to go?' Pasha asked quietly.

'I'm sorry, Pasha,' Miss Cuneen said, and she really did sound sorry. 'When his case last came up before the committee, they decided that he should go to the Farrells. We can't change that.'

'Why can't he stay with us?' Mammy Tallon asked.

There was silence for a moment, broken in the end by Father Shanahan. 'I can appreciate and admire your concern, Mrs Pasha, but the best interest of Loughlin must be the top priority,' he said.

'That's our priority too,' Pasha said.

Again there was silence.

'I'm sorry, Pasha and Mrs Pasha,' said Guard Mitchell. 'But once the Health Board has made a decision it's my job to see that it is carried out. If they say he goes to the Farrells, then he goes to the Farrells.'

Dadge jumped across to the table and caught Lockie's arm. Before anyone could move he had hauled the boy out and placed him in the corner by the window. He stood in front of the astonished boy and raised his fists as he had done when he faced the farmer, Peter Murtagh, at Ballysteen.

'He is not going!' Dadge said angrily. 'He is not! No way is he going! Over my dead body is he going to that house!'

Pasha stood up and went to Dadge. He stood before him and held his two hands up, palms forward.

'Easy, Dadge,' he said. 'Easy. There's no point in trying to stop them. Let it be.'

'Pasha, you're not going to give in to them,' Dadge said in disbelief. 'You're not going to let them take him back.'

'We can't stop them.'

'Let it be, Dadge,' Mammy Tallon said. 'For now at any rate.'

Dadge stopped and looked at her. Her face was calm. It was impossible to make out from her expression what she meant by 'for now at any rate'. Pasha nodded to him and he lowered his fists. He bowed his head and strode to the door and out.

Lockie too wondered what Mammy Tallon meant. Later, when Miss Cuneen said that they must leave, he was not as sad as he might otherwise have been because of the faint hope raised by that 'for now'.

Lockie tried hard not to show his feelings when saying goodbye. It was not so hard when shaking hands with Pasha. Lockie knew that he wouldn't like crying and that kind of stuff. Pasha held his hand for a while and Lockie's eyes brightened when he felt a crisp, folded piece of paper pressed against his palm. He guessed that it was a note, and he stowed it in his pocket to read later on.

Mammy Tallon threw her arms around him and pressed him close. When she let him go, his face was twisted in the effort to hold back his tears.

Dadge was nowhere to be seen. When he left the caravan, he had vanished and had not been seen since. The priest and the guard had already gone, walking back to the village. Miss Cuneen sat in the car while Lockie was saying goodbye to the others. Zack and Katy came out of their caravan and each of them gave him a pound.

'Sorry, Lockie,' Katy said in a whisper, and tears shone in the corners of her eyes.

As they drove away, Dadge appeared. He stepped around a corner of the dodgem tent and ran to the car. Miss Cuneen stopped and Lockie lowered the window at his side.

Dadge handed him a white plastic bag. 'Something for the road,' he said and walked away without another word. Lockie looked in the bag. It contained three rosy apples and two eggs. The eggs were still hot from the water they were boiled in.

As they drove north along the coast road from Coonmore,

Lockie remembered the note given to him by Pasha. He took it out to read, but it wasn't a message; it was a ten-pound note. He burst into tears and cried quietly.

They went through places that were familiar to Lockie from a few short weeks before when he travelled through them on the cart with Dadge and Rosie. At Coonmore Miss Cuneen treated him to ice-cream and Coke at a café. Beyond Coonmore they took the coast road and had a sight of the sea. It reminded Lockie of his recent break for freedom.

They spoke little on the journey. Lockie was down-hearted. He suspected that Miss Cuneen felt the same way. She had no choice but to bring him back.

When they turned into the drab terrace where the Farrells lived, Lockie's spirits dropped even lower. It was almost a physical pain.

'Well, now, Lockie, me hearty,' John Farrell greeted him cheerily. 'Abandoned ship, did we? Never mind. Back aboard and the past is forgotten.'

Rita Farrell was not as breezy as her husband. 'You're welcome home, Lockie,' she said. 'I hope you won't be so wayward this time, and that you'll learn to fall in with the rest of us. We'll do all we can for you.'

Her glasses flashed, and Lockie couldn't see her eyes.

Miss Cuneen said her goodbyes.

'I'll leave you my address, Lockie,' she said. 'As you know, I must call once every six months on behalf of the Health Board to see how you're getting on, but if you ever need to talk to me, be sure to write and I'll come.'

'Thanks,' was all Lockie could say. She had never said anything like that to him before, so why did she say it now? Maybe what she was saying was as much for the Farrells' information as it was for Lockie.

CHAPTER FOURTEEN

A Berth Aloft

Lockie's life in the Farrell household entered its second phase. It changed a little from his first sojourn there. Now he had even less freedom. Rita Farrell met him every afternoon at the school gate, and, when he got home, he was not allowed out again. He no longer ran errands to the shop or the post office.

Every Sunday they visited the old ship, *The Golden Albatross*, tied up at the pier. Lockie soon grew tired of going there Sunday after Sunday. True, it was a beautiful old ship, the planks of the deck honey-coloured and shining, the panels and timber mouldings of the bridge dark and smooth, the three masts with their network of spars and ropes rising from the deck.

From John Farrell, Lockie had picked up names like 'fore mast', 'main mast', 'mizen mast', and he knew where the 'forecastle' was, and the 'quarterdeck', and 'amidships', and 'port' and 'starboard'. The most interesting thing for him was the ship's compass housed in the binnacle on the bridge. He asked Mr Farrell to explain how they navigated by it.

'Too complicated for a landlubber like yourself,' he said. 'Wait until you've found your sea legs and we'll give you a run-down on it.' Lockie suspected that navigation was as great a mystery to John Farrell as it was to himself.

He thought often of Pasha and Mammy Tallon and of Dadge. For a short time he had known a freedom and companionship that had never before been part of his life.

He lay awake at night, thinking. The more he thought about it, the more he realised how few friends he had. If you left out Pasha and Mammy Tallon, Dadge and Mickey Wheeler, the rest were either enemies or uncaring strangers. Then he corrected himself. Miss Cuneen was okay too, and so were Job and Moll and Zack. Maybe even Katy wasn't too bad.

'Wash up now, Lockie,' Rita Farrell ordered after dinner one evening. But it was time for Lockie to light his short fuse once again.

'Why does it always have to be me?' he asked. 'Let someone else do it for a change.'

Mr Farrell was reading the evening paper by the fire. He dropped the paper and caught Lockie by the back of his jumper and lifted him off the ground.

'What have we here?' he bellowed. 'Mutiny, is it? Is it?'

'No, Cap'n,' Lockie said, hoping that calling him 'Captain' would soften his heart. But his grovelling was in vain. He was frogmarched to 'the galley' and forced to comply with the 'first mate's' request. When he had finished that chore, he was ordered to wash the milk bottles and put them outside the door for the milkman.

Again he did as ordered, but this time he bolted. When he had placed the milk bottles on the doorstep, he pulled the door shut behind him and ran. It was dark and the street lights were on. He ran towards the Coonmore road. Several people spoke to him. One old man said, 'What's the hurry, boy? Where are you off to?'

He was glad when he had left the street lights and pedestrians behind. Out on the Coonmore road the traffic was heavy, cars mainly, with blinding headlights. They forced him to take to the grass margin, and he ran as fast as he could along the margin in the direction of Coonmore.

Pasha and Mammy Tallon wouldn't be there, he knew, but if he could find somewhere to spend the night, he would head for the fairground in Kiltarr in the morning. If he had any luck, he would make the fair in three days at most. He might even be able to thumb a lift.

A good idea! There was nothing to stop him from doing it now. It was just a matter of finding the best place, not at a turn or at a narrow part of the road. It had to be at a place where a driver wouldn't mind stopping.

Then he found an ideal spot, outside a filling station. The road widened there, and the place was well lit. A few cars sped past, ignoring his thumb as it drew extravagant arcs in the air. At last a car stopped, and he felt sick with disappointment. It had a flashing blue light on its roof, and a garda stepped out.

'Come on, Lockie,' he said. 'We'll bring you home.'

'How do you know who I am?' Lockie asked.

The garda laughed. 'Hop in there, and you'll be okay,' he said.

Rita Farrell gave him a lecture when he got home. 'You're impossible. What can we do with you? We really are doing our best, giving you the kind of upbringing that will make a man of you, and look at how you thank us for it.'

'I'll go again,' Lockie said.

John Farrell came and stood over him, glaring down at him. 'You'll do what?'

'I'll run away again. I don't care how many times I'm brought back, I'll run away again.'

'No, you won't, and I'll see to it that you don't!'

Mr Farrell took the stepladder from its place under the stairs, and he stood it under the trapdoor in the landing ceiling. Gordon and Ruthie were already in bed. Lockie and Mrs Farrell sat in the living-room, listening to him fumbling in the attic and going up and down the ladder. When he returned to the living-room, he was red-faced from his exertions.

'Now, young fellow-me-lad,' he said to Lockie, 'from here on you're going to sleep aloft. We'll see how you can get out of that.'

So Lockie was banished to the attic. It had been floored with loose planks, and most of the space up there was used for storage, with cardboard boxes everywhere. In the centre, on the floor, was a bed – the mattress from Lockie's bunk and some bedclothes.

The trapdoor was left open to allow light from the landing into the attic. When Lockie had undressed and gone under the bedclothes, John Farrell's head appeared through the opening.

'Battening down the hatches now,' he said, 'and removing the companion-way.'

His head disappeared and Lockie heard the clunk of the trapdoor being dropped into place and the ladder being folded and laid against the wall. It was dark as tar.

Later the Farrells went to bed, and Lockie could hear them speaking. They mustn't have realised that their voices carried much more easily through the ceiling than through the bedroom walls. He could hear every word they said. They seemed to be continuing a conversation that had begun downstairs.

'Why can't we ask the Health Board to take him away?' Rita Farrell was saying.

'Because they would see that as failure on our part,' her husband answered.

'What about the other people he was with?'

'I was talking to the Malones and the Cagneys. They weren't given a child to replace him. The Board takes a poor view of a family giving a child back.'

'All right, then. Why can't we do without him?'

'Doing without him would be no trouble. Doing without the grant would be something else. Things are tight enough already.'

'So we're stuck with him?'

'Looks like it.'

They were silent for a while. Then Rita Farrell spoke. 'He says he'll run away again.'

'We'll just have to keep a closer watch on him. At least while he's sleeping in the attic, he can't make off during the night.'

CHAPTER FIFTEEN

Another Bid for Freedom

Lockie lay on his bed aloft. He didn't sleep. The events of the evening were still too fresh in his mind.

In the small hours the moon came out and a shaft of its pale light slanted from the skylight past the foot of his pallet and fell on a wooden box, a kind of ancient sea chest with a hinged cover. He got out of bed and raised the cover. The chest contained an old sailor's coat and cap, and a number of books.

The coat and cap were a little large for him, but he tried them on and they felt comfortable. There wasn't enough light to read the books, but one of them looked like a ledger with old handwriting. When he had emptied the box, he put it under the skylight, and stood on it. He opened the skylight and put his head and shoulders out in the open air.

It was chilly, and he was glad of the sailor's thick coat. But there was a marvellous sense of being alone and free, looking over the roofs of the houses all around him, and over the houses stepping down the hill towards the shore. Here and there yellow street lamps spread their colour on the house-tops as if a yellow dye had been spilled over the whole town.

He could see the water, dark as ink except where lights at the end of the pier were reflected, rocking gently on the ripples of a calm sea.

'Captain Bligh thinks this is a kind of a jail,' he said to himself, 'but it's not. It's a place to be free. I'm away from them all.' He looked down and said, 'This is my world, and you're all barred from it.'

Without realising it, he had been speaking aloud, but not loudly enough to be heard in the rooms below. He had marked out his territory. They could order him about when he was down among them, but up here he was king.

'How was it in the crow's nest?' John Farrell asked him in the morning.

'Not great,' Lockie lied. He was afraid that if he said otherwise, Captain Bligh might bring him down again.

Every night Lockie looked forward to going to bed. He didn't let on because they might become suspicious. He pretended that he really didn't want to go when John ordered him aloft every night. The attic became as familiar to him as any room downstairs, and in a short time he was able to move around there in total darkness. Even when the moon was hidden, there was a faint glow as the street lamps cast their yellow light on the underside of the clouds.

On moonless nights he liked to lie on the bed and watch the stars through the skylight. They reminded him of the nights he had spent in the open air in Dadge's old sleeping-bag. Were it not for the nights in the attic, Lockie would probably have tried to run away again.

Sometimes he saw ships passing in the night. He couldn't make out their shapes, but he could guess their size from the galaxy of glittering lights that moved slowly across the horizon.

Now and then a distant droning heralded a plane and his eyes scanned the sky in search of it. Invariably he found it, a moving star following a straight path across the sky through the fixed stars of the night.

At the end of August he was back at school. Sometimes Rita Farrell took them through the park on the way home. Gordon had even begun to show an interest in the ducks on the pond.

One day Lockie was startled by something hissing at him in the shrubbery. He looked but couldn't see what it was. He heard it again: 'H-s-s-s-t!'

Slowly and cautiously he approached the bush, a large laurel at the side of the path.

'Stand there now!' a voice spoke out of the bush. He stopped and looked at Gordon and Rita. They were by the pond, looking at the ducks.

'Turn your back and pretend you're looking around,' the voice continued.

'Dadge!' Lockie blurted out. He recognised the voice and only Dadge could have told him to pretend he was looking around. He didn't have to pretend. What else could he do if he were to stand by the bush and listen?

'Just one word,' the voice said. 'What room are you sleeping in?'

'What?'

'Never mind your "what". Tell me and go away. We don't want anyone to see us talking.'

'There's no one around.'

'Will you tell me and go. Which room?'

'No room. I'm in the attic.'

A rustling sound came from the bush.

'Dadge?'

No answer.

'Dadge.'

No answer. He was gone. What had he in mind? A rescue? Would he do it off his own bat? Was Pasha or Mammy Tallon in on it? A wild hope took hold of Lockie as he went home. Dadge could have come out and spoken to him in a normal way, but no! With Dadge everything had to be dramatic.

That night everybody was in bed and probably asleep, but Lockie was still on his nightly vigil, standing on the box, his head and shoulders through the skylight, his elbows resting on the slates as he gazed in the direction of the sea. A faint click at the gutter drew his attention, and he saw the sides of a ladder resting against it.

A moment later and a head wearing a cap appeared.

'That you, Dadge?' Lockie whispered.

'You're there? Good. I thought I'd have to go up the roof to the skylight. Can you get out?'

'I can.'

'It's a cold night. Have you something warm to wear?'

Lockie assured him that he was well dressed for a night journey. He had the sailor's coat and cap and he hadn't yet undressed for bed. He squirmed through the skylight and got out on the roof. As he did so, his shoes made a light clicking sound against the frame of the skylight.

'Take off them shoes! You'll wake the whole town!' Dadge warned.

Lockie did as he was bid, tied the laces together, and slung the shoes around his neck. When he had edged down to the ladder, Dadge helped him turn around and place his foot on a rung. They got down safely and Lockie put his shoes back on.

'What about the ladder?' Lockie asked.

'They won't find it until morning.'

'Who owns it?'

'Don't know. I found it lying by that new building up the street. Come on this way.'

They went through several streets and came to the school. A white van was parked outside.

'This is it,' Dadge said. 'Hop in.'

Lockie got in the passenger side and Dadge sat at the wheel. They took off with a few mighty leaps forward, and when the van steadied they drove for nearly a hundred yards in first gear, the engine racing loudly. To the sleepers in the houses by the road they must have sounded like a tractor.

Then they went for ages in second, until, with a mighty grinding of gears, Dadge changed up to third. He drove the van out of the town and down the Coonmore road. Soon they turned on to a byroad.

'Where did you get the van?' Lockie asked.

'Friends. Borrowed it. You'll meet them soon. They're minding Rosie for me. They know you. At least one of them said he did.'

'Where's Pasha and Mammy Tallon?'

'Gone to Tallon Island. They're waiting for us there.'

'But how are we going to get there? I'll be caught again and sent back to that place,' Lockie whined.

'Don't worry. We'll get you to Tallon Island all right.'

'Who's we?'

'Questions. Questions!' Dadge said, and he sounded impatient. 'Can't you stay quiet. I'm not used to driving vans. I have to keep my mind on it.'

CHAPTER SIXTEEN

Travelling Clan

They came to the top of a hill. The fence on the right-hand side was back from the road, and on the wide, grassy margin stood a caravan. They pulled in beside the caravan. The top half of the caravan door opened and a dark shaggy head looked out over the half-door.

'That you, Dadge?' a gravelly voice inquired.

'Me, Tom. Who else?' Dadge answered.

'Did you get him?'

'He's here.'

Another head appeared, dark too, but showing at a lower level than the first. 'Hey, Lockie!' it said.

Lockie recognised the voice at once – Mickey Wheeler, his friend from the school in Cloughlee.

'Hey, Mickey,' he said, delighted.

'Come on in,' the first voice said. 'You're welcome, young Lockie.'

The interior was slightly different from when Lockie last saw it. A curtain had been pulled across at one end, but a corner of it was lifted and three small faces peeped out, Kitty, Tommy, and Molly.

A door at the other end was open and a woman with fair hair stood there. She was pulling on a jumper.

'Come in, come in,' she said as her head emerged out of the jumper. She had a handsome face with high cheekbones, and her hair was parted at the centre and cascaded down over her shoulders. She was tying it at the back of her head with a green ribbon, but she did so hurriedly and a few wisps remained loose, hanging down in front of her right ear.

'I'll make a sup of tea,' she said. She pronounced it 'tay'.

'Not for me,' Dadge said. 'I must be on my way. I'd like to be a long way from here by the morning. When the word is out that Lockie here is gone, I'll be the first one they'll ask about him.'

'Thanks, Dadge,' Lockie said, 'for getting me out. When are you coming back for me?'

'I'm not coming back for you,' Dadge said. 'Tom Wheeler here will get you down to Tallon Island. You'll be safe with him.'

He walked out the door, and Mickey's father, Tom, went with him. As they went out, Tom said: 'The jennet is tied to the tree. I tackled her up just before you came back.'

'You hungry?' the woman asked Lockie.

'No, thank you, Mrs Wheeler,' Lockie said. He was too excited to think of food.

'Don't mind your "Mrs Wheeler",' she said. 'If you're going to be one of the family for a while, you'll have to drop that.'

'What should I call you, then?' Lockie asked.

'Call me by my name – Julia.'

'What does Mickey call you?'

'He calls her Julia,' a voice from behind the curtain piped up. 'We all call her Julia.'

'Go to sleep, Kitty,' Julia called to her. 'Don't keep Tommy and Molly awake.'

Julia smiled. 'They're excited because a stranger's here,' she said, her voice lowered so that the young children wouldn't hear.

Tom Wheeler came back. 'He's on his way,' he said. 'A true blue is our friend, Dadge. When he's on your side, he'd go through the fires of hell for you.'

'Can I ask you something?' Lockie said.

'Ask away, boy.'

Lockie got a good look at him at last. His face was almost jet black from the half inch of black stubble that covered his chin and jaws. When he smiled at Lockie, his teeth gleamed.

'Why is it going to take six weeks to get to Tallon Island? Aren't we going in the van?'

'We are. True for you. And six weeks is a long time to do a journey that should take us only half a day. But we have calls to make and business to do in places along the way.'

'Oh,' Lockie said, satisfied with the explanation.

'Will we go to bed now?' Mickey asked.

'Yes, off you go,' Julia said. 'Have you a night shirt, Lockie?'

'No,' Lockie said. 'I have only what I'm wearing.'

Julia opened the door on the left at the back and stepped inside. She brought out a large striped shirt and gave it to Lockie.

'Here,' she said, 'wear that for a night-shirt.'

'Come on, Lockie,' Mickey said. 'We're in here.' He spoke gleefully, delighted to have Lockie for company. He opened the door to the right at the back and Lockie followed him into the tiny compartment.

There was hardly room to turn around: two bunks on one

side and hooks on the wall opposite for their clothing, nothing else. A window on the end wall was small and the top part was opened out about four inches. There was no light, so they left the door slightly ajar while they undressed and got into bed.

'Which do you want, Lockie, top or bottom?' Mickey asked.

'I don't mind,' Lockie said. 'Which would you like?'

'Tell you what: I'll turn around and hold up my fingers. You guess how many fingers I have up, and if you guess the right number, you can have the bottom.'

'Wouldn't it be better if I had my choice?'

'Okay so. You guess the right number and you can have any bunk you want.'

Mickey turned around and Lockie guessed seven. Mickey turned back and yes, he had raised seven fingers.

'Okay,' said Lockie, 'I'll take the top one.'

Both of them laughed loudly. They clambered into the bunks.

But they didn't go to sleep straight away. Lockie told Mickey all that had happened to him since they last met. When he came to the part about Moll Diggin capturing the thief and catching him by the hair, Mickey laughed uproariously.

Julia knocked at the door and said: 'Go to sleep now. We're moving out.'

'Are we going now, in the night?' Lockie whispered.

'Yes.'

'While we're in bed?'

'Yes.'

'But it'll keep us awake!'

'Naw! Puts you to sleep,' Mickey assured him.

'Good night!'

'Sleep tight!'

Lockie stayed awake for a while. He heard Tom Wheeler go out and close the door. The caravan jerked slightly and there was a metallic sound as Tom attached it to the tow bar on the van. Then the door of the van opened and closed again. The engine started and the caravan rolled forward, lurching slightly as it moved out of the grass margin on to the hard surface of the road.

The journey through the night was uneventful. Tom Wheeler drove slowly, and the hum of the van engine and the gentle rocking of the caravan soon made Lockie feel drowsy. He asked sleepily, 'Why does he go at night?'

'No traffic, no cops,' Mickey said.

Soon they turned off the byroad on to one of the main roads. Lockie knew because the caravan moved more smoothly. Now and again it swayed as some heavy truck thundered by with a roar of engine and a swish of air. Mickey was first to fall asleep, and not long after that Lockie too fell into a deep dreamless sleep.

CHAPTER SEVENTEEN

On the Road Again

Loud voices and the noise of car and van engines running in high gear wakened Lockie. The van was not moving.

He looked out the window. Their caravan was parked with others at the side of a field. Caravans just newly arrived were being towed into position. The drivers were guided by people on the ground: 'Back up a small bit! Steady on there now!' The Wheelers' caravan was third from the road.

It was early morning. Mickey and Lockie got up, and after breakfast asked Julia if they could go up the town. Julia thought for a while.

'All right,' she said eventually, 'but don't do anything to draw attention to ye. The hunt for Lockie might be in full swing.'

The boys strolled up the main street of the small town, past the sign which said 'Welcome to Butlersbridge!' The street was crowded, little groups standing, gossiping, here and there. Near the crossroads at the entrance to the town larger groups stood around, looking at horses and ponies of various sizes and colours.

'What's on?' Lockie asked.

'It's the horse fair,' Mickey said.

≈　　　≈　　　≈

Next morning the two boys went up town to see the fair. At the crossroads a crowd was gathered and Mickey said, 'Let's watch. They're making a deal.'

They stood at the edge of the crowd listening to a horse owner and a man in riding breeches arguing about the price of a black pony. After a lot of shouting and back slapping and walking up and down the bargain was made and the crowd began to scatter again.

'Lockie, come away,' Mickey whispered and he slipped out of the crowd and hurried towards a side road. Lockie followed, wondering why the haste. When they got clear of the crowd, Mickey took to his heels and scampered up a back lane, before turning towards the main street again. They stopped near the church. Mickey peeped around the corner.

'What's going on?' Lockie asked him.

'Didn't you see the guard?' Mickey said.

'No. What guard?'

'The guard standing at the corner. He kept looking at you. I'm afraid he knows about you.'

'What are we going to do?' Lockie asked, and he sounded scared.

'We'll go back by the fields so he won't know what caravan we're in.'

They went back to the caravan site by a roundabout way through the fields, and arrived close to the caravan, but in the field next to it. Voices could be heard at the other side of the Wheelers' caravan, so Mickey motioned to Lockie, and they ducked down behind the fence. They peeped through gaps in a thorn bush.

Tom and Julia Wheeler were standing there, talking to two guards. Mickey whispered, 'The thin one is the one who was sizing you up at the fair.'

Tom was speaking: 'A pale young fellow, you say.' They could hear him quite distinctly from where they lay.

'Yes, about twelve years old,' a guard said.

'No sign of any young fellow on the road anywhere on the journey down,' Tom said. 'If we came on a young fellow out on the road at that time of night, we'd have picked him up, especially a fellow as young as that.'

'You sure?' the guard asked.

'Of course, I'm sure,' Tom said indignantly. 'I saw no pale young fellow on the road. No, nor a young fellow of any other complexion either.'

'Would you mind if we searched the caravan?'

'No. Search away!'

The gardaí went into the caravan and came out almost at once. They were apparently satisfied that no one was in the caravan, other than the three young children.

The guards returned to their car and drove off, the blue lights blinking on the roof. The boys waited until the car had vanished around the turn of the road a good half mile away before they came out and joined the others.

'What'll we do now?' Tom said.

'I think he should move to Barrymore tonight,' Julia replied.

Tom agreed. 'Those guards are like Kerry Blues,' he said. 'When they get a sniff of something, they keep worrying it until they have it torn asunder.'

'Where will we go in Barrymore?' Lockie asked.

'Don't worry your head, boy,' Tom reassured him. 'The plan was to bring you to a friend of Pasha's, Mike Donovan, and he would get you to the island. I know where he lives, about a mile out on the Skeheen road from Barrymore. There was no day fixed, so you'll be all right.'

CHAPTER EIGHTEEN

Parting with Old Friends

Mickey didn't come out of the bedroom to say goodbye to Lockie that night. But as Tom Wheeler and Lockie were moving away in the van, he came to the door and waved. Then he turned quickly and rushed back inside.

'He'll be lonesome after you,' Tom said.

Lockie was dumb. He was close to tears.

'Bed-time for all good policemen,' Tom said as they passed through the silent town.

They travelled on byroads most of the way, except for one short stretch of the main road between Duncarney and Derreenbrack, and arrived in Skeheen at about three o'clock in the morning. Lockie slept for the greater part of the journey, waking up when they slowed as they went through the deserted towns.

'We won't be long now,' Tom said as they left Skeheen. About ten minutes later they turned off the road and drove up a narrow boreen to a long, ivy-clad farmhouse. Tom got out and knocked at the door. The knocker sounded very loud in the quiet of the night.

A light came on in an upstairs window and Lockie heard

the sound of the window being raised.

'Who's there? a voice asked.

'It's Tom Wheeler. I'm bringing the young fellow for Pasha.'

'Hold on a minute,' the voice said, and the window was slammed shut.

A short time later lights came on downstairs and the front door was opened. Lockie got out and he and Tom were invited into the house. They were led into the kitchen. The grey-haired man who let them in was barefoot, dressed in trousers and shirt only. A woman about the same age, wearing a dressing-gown, came in.

She went to Lockie and ran her hand through his hair. 'So you're the lad they want to keep away from Pasha!' she said kindly.

'Ye must be hungry and tired,' the man said. 'Put on the kettle, Sarah,' he said. 'I'll get the fire going.'

'Don't bother about me, Mike,' Tom said. 'I must be on my way. I want to get back before daylight.'

He turned to Lockie. 'Good luck to you, Lockie boy. Tell Pasha and Mammy Tallon and Dadge I was asking for them. You'll give them a good account of us, I hope.'

Lockie found it hard to say what he felt, how grateful he was to the Wheelers, how he was going to miss Mickey, how he loved the freedom of life in the caravan.

'Thanks, Tom,' was all he could manage.

It was noon before Lockie woke next day in a large soft bed. In the afternoon he went out to the strand, because Mike told him Pasha would come for him there. He was impatient, gazing out to sea in the hope of seeing Pasha's boat coming.

A boat, tiny in the distance, came around the headland at

the northern point of Seal Island, the island closest to shore. It was too small to make out the colour or how many people were in it. Gradually it grew larger and seemed to be making for the strand. As it came bouncing over the waves towards them, Lockie could see two people on board.

'Here he comes,' Mike said. 'And Dadge is with him.'

'How can you tell from here?' Lockie asked in surprise.

'A boat making straight for the strand, two people in it,' Mike said. 'Who else could it be?'

Mike was right. The engine was cut, and when the bow of the boat touched the shore, Pasha and Dadge jumped out and hauled her up on the shingle, above the line of dried seaweed which marked high-water at the last full tide.

'You were out in the sun,' Dadge said to Lockie. 'You're a better colour now than when I saw your head sticking out the skylight, just a few days ago.'

Pasha said nothing, just smiled and put out his hand to catch Lockie's in a firm, warm grip. They went up to Mike's house where Sarah greeted them.

Soon Dadge said it was time for him to be tackling up.

'Where are you going?' Lockie asked. He thought Dadge was to be one of the new family in Tallon Island, the family of Pasha, Mammy Tallon, Lockie and Dadge.

'Why don't you stay on Tallon Island?' Lockie asked him.

'Ah, you know me,' Dadge said. 'The only place for me is the open road. I can't stand houses, or being in one place all the time. Already I've been anchored in the island for longer than I was any place in a long time.'

Lockie went to the field with him to catch Rosie. The jennet came up to her master and he fondled her head, rubbing her ears and her mane, and cooing to her as if she were a young child.

They brought her back to the farmyard and Dadge tackled her to the cart. Mike and Pasha had come out, and Sarah stood in the doorway.

'Remember, Dadge,' Pasha said to him, 'there'll always be a place for you with us on the island. Don't forget to call to the house in Coonmore and see that everything is okay. If you're there next winter, we might see you.'

'God speed!' Mike Donovan said.

'Goodbye, Dadge,' was all Lockie could mutter. People were constantly moving out of his world. More and more, Pasha and Mammy Tallon were becoming the only fixtures in his life.

Dadge shook the reins and the jennet began to move towards the gate.

'Hup there now, Rosie my girl. Let's get to blazes outa here!' he said. He took off his cap and waved it first at Sarah, then at the others. He went out the gate and, as soon as the jennet felt the hard road under her feet, she broke into a canter, as if she were delighted to be on the move again.

CHAPTER NINETEEN

Tallon Island

'Time for us to be moving too,' Pasha said. 'I'm very thankful to you, Mike. I know I can rely on you not to say anything about our young boy here.'

'No one will hear a word from us,' Mike said. 'But what about the crowd on the island?'

'The island people will be okay. They won't tell anyone. They all know he's coming and why. If we got a few years out of it, he'd be older and there would be no good reason to send him back to that crowd again.'

They went down to the strand. Lockie and Pasha went aboard and Mike pushed the boat away from the shore. Pasha shipped the oars and went to the stern. He raised the outboard motor until the propellor was in the water. He pulled the cord and the engine spluttered. It did so again and again. Eventually it started and the boat suddenly surged forward, throwing Lockie back off the seat. He hauled himself up again.

'You all right?' Pasha asked.

'Fine,' Lockie said.

The boat bounced over the waves. As they moved out of

the lee of Seal Island, the bow rose before them, riding over the higher waves that ran there. Lockie was scared at first, but when he looked at Pasha sitting calm and relaxed in the stern, he was reassured.

Pasha wore a rough, tweed jacket and trousers of the same material but a different colour. Under the jacket he had a high-necked, blue jumper. His cap was low on his forehead and he squinted as he peered into the wind.

'Tallon ahead,' Pasha said, and Lockie looked to where he was pointing.

'How long till we get there?' Lockie asked.

'About half an hour in this sea,' Pasha said.

They didn't speak again until they were approaching the island. The sea had calmed a little by then.

'She's waiting for us,' Pasha said.

Lockie squinted and stared through the spray being thrown up over the bow by the wind. He could see a concrete pier jutting out into the sea, and on it there was the hint of a person, but, if Pasha hadn't said so, he wouldn't have known it was Mammy Tallon. They came closer.

Mammy Tallon was wearing a dark brown coat and a blue head scarf. She waved at them and they both waved back. Pasha cut the engine and let the boat drift close to the steps of the pier. He jumped out and held the boat steady.

Lockie got out, ran up the steps and threw his arms around Mammy Tallon.

'Stop your old nonsense,' she said, but she hugged him nevertheless.

They left the pier and turned on to a grass path which soon developed into a gravelly boreen. At the end of the boreen they came through a gate to a narrow road, not much used to judge by the line of grass along the centre. Dried cakes of cow dung here and there suggested a cattle path.

They had been walking uphill from the time they left the pier, and they were now high above the sea. The view was splendid. Between the island and the mainland the sea was blue, flecked with little white breakers. Green islands sat among the breakers, and beyond the islands the mainland provided a backdrop of dark blue hills.

The hill sloped upward on their right-hand side, and the island stretched away to the south, a patchwork of small fields bound by stone-wall fences. It was almost totally bare of trees. In the distance two houses were surrounded by bushes of some kind, but a two-storey house much nearer was built of dark stone. A wreath of whitish smoke rose from the chimney at the near end and drifted towards them.

'What's that nice smell?' Lockie asked.

'Turf smoke,' Mammy Tallon said. 'That's one of the things I miss when I'm away from here.'

They turned in the gateway. Mammy Tallon raised the latch on the front door and went in.

'It wasn't locked while you were out!' Lockie said in amazement.

'No, it wasn't. There's no need for locks on Tallon Island.'

'And no need for you to be afraid,' Pasha said. 'You're safe on Tallon Island. The people here are friends.'

'How many people are there?' Lockie asked.

'I don't know. I never counted,' Mammy Tallon said. There must be a hundred or a hundred and fifty all told. Now you make one more, and you're welcome, Lockie! Isn't he welcome, Pasha?'

'Welcome a hundred thousand times.'

'Thank you,' Lockie said. 'Thanks a million for bringing me here to your house.'

'Wait until you're here for a while before you start thanking us. Maybe when you start helping in the house and on the land, and doing a bit of work around the place, you might be singing a different tune. Remember that we've adopted you. Maybe *they* don't think so, but what *they* think makes no difference here.'

The front door opened straight into a large room, a room where Lockie felt instantly at home. A bright fire burned in the grate. Against the wall facing the fire was a dresser full of gleaming plates, saucers, dishes, and cups and jugs hanging from a line of hooks.

A radio sat on the back window sill, and a great clock hung on the wall beside the front window. The face had gone yellow and it had roman numerals. It had a slow, heavy tick that beat out time, though time seemed to stand still there in the peace and quiet.

'I like it here,' Lockie said.

'Come on, let me show you your bedroom,' Mammy Tallon said, and she went ahead of him up the stairs. Three doors led out of the large landing.

'In here,' Mammy Tallon said, and she showed Lockie into the room on the right.

It was a large room with two beds. Lockie chose the one near the front window, the window with a view of the sea. The floor was covered with a pale blue lino and a white sheepskin rug was placed beside the bed. The ceiling sloped at both sides down to the tops of the windows.

'This is my room, just mine?' Lockie asked.

'Your very own, but if Dadge stays with us for a few days at Christmas, we'll let him have the other bed.'

'I never had a room to myself before. This is great!'

CHAPTER TWENTY

A New Life

They had tea, and, to celebrate Lockie's arrival, Mammy Tallon baked a currant cake. Afterwards Lockie went out with Pasha to milk the cow, and his life on the island began.

In the yard a few hens ambled around pecking the ground. Lockie looked in the hen-house and in the shed which held the garden tools. The motorbike was there, raised on its stand, its handlebars gleaming. One end of the shed was partitioned off for the cow.

'Why isn't the cow in there now?' Lockie asked when he came out.

'The weather is too fine. We put her in there at night only in the cold in the middle of winter. Some winters, if the weather is mild, we don't put her in at all.'

They walked up to the top of the hill behind the house. The fields on the other side sloped down to the sea, and about three-quarters of the way down was the village, a cluster of houses perched on the side of the hill.

Pasha paused and squinted against the sunlight. 'It doesn't look too bad,' he said. 'We might be able to go out tomorrow.'

'Out where?'

'Fishing.'

'Who? You and me?'

'You can come along,' Pasha said. 'I go out with a few fellows from the village.'

They found the cow, a black and white Friesian, behind the wall of the next field. She stood while Pasha sat on his heels beside her and milked her into the bucket. Lockie watched enthralled.

'Can I milk her?' he asked.

'Come here, and try it.'

Pasha held the bucket while Lockie tugged at the cow's teats. He tugged with all his might but he failed to produce milk.

'Squeeze and pull down gently at the same time,' Pasha told him.

Eventually he managed to squirt a weak jet of milk into the bucket.

'You'll learn,' Pasha said, and he took over and completed the job.

Later Lockie went out with Mammy Tallon to lock in the hens. They were all inside sitting on the bars and she closed the door and put a peg through a hole in the bolt.

'Those foxes are clever devils,' Mammy Tallon said. 'They are crafty enough to pull back the bolt if you don't secure it.'

When they went inside, Pasha was lighting the oil lamp. There was no electricity on that side of the island.

'It would cost too much,' Pasha said. 'They want me to pay for the poles and the wire to bring it up from the village.'

'And pay for their electricity after that,' Mammy Tallon added.

They sat by the turf fire then, listening to Lockie's stories of his adventures since he left them at the funfair in Kiltarr. They had no television, but they had a radio, which they turned on to hear the news and the weather forecast. The forecast was good for the south west.

'We'd better go to bed,' Pasha said. 'We have an early start in the morning.'

Lockie got into bed, feeling tired. It had been a long day, and he had had little sleep on the previous night. When he lay down he could see sky and sea through the window, a pale blue sprinkled with stars, and below it the darker blue, almost black, of the sea.

The sound of the sea was soothing. He was almost content, but a small fear niggled. How long before *they* find me again? he wondered.

≋　　　≋　　　≋

Lockie woke in the morning to the sound of Pasha's voice, 'Come on, Lockie. Time to go to the strand.'

He jumped out of bed and looked out the window. It was a fine morning, the sun rising in a clear sky, the sea calmer than it was the day before. The white horses were fewer and tamer.

Through the back window he saw Mammy Tallon coming from the hen-house, carrying a basin. The hens were pecking madly at whatever it was she had thrown on the ground for them. The best time of the day, Dadge had called it once, and he was right.

Downstairs, after a hurried breakfast, Lockie was ready to go with Pasha to the strand. Mammy Tallon fussed around him, getting him to put on his overcoat, and she gave him a woollen cap, brown with yellow patterns in circles around it.

'Put that on when you get in the boat,' she said. 'It can be very cold when you're out on the water.'

When Pasha and Lockie got to the strand, only one of the crew was there before them.

'Good morning, Jack,' Pasha called out as they approached.

Jack looked around. He had a chubby face with a quarter-inch of black stubble mingled with grey all over his jaw. He too was wearing a cap.

The boat was pulled up on the strand. It was a yellow, clinker-built timber boat with a brown gunwale. It was about thirty feet long and had three sets of oarlocks on each side.

Jack looked at Lockie. 'I see you brought some help, Pasha,' he said.

'This is Lockie,' Pasha told him.

'Ho there, Lockie. You're coming out for a bit of fishing?' Lockie nodded.

'The net in order?' Pasha asked.

'Yes. Here comes Gerry.'

The man who joined them then was much younger than the other two. He put out his hand and said, 'You're welcome, Lockie. Going to join the crew?'

Lockie said, 'Yes.' He wondered how Gerry knew his name, but guessed that Pasha must have spoken about him.

Lockie was told to get in the boat and sit at the stern. When the boat was afloat and all were aboard, the three men took the oars and began to row together in harmony. She cut through the smooth water at a gentle pace.

The others faced Lockie, Gerry nearest, then Jack and Pasha at the bow. Gerry set the rudder in position, and pushed the tiller through the slot at the top. He told Lockie to take the tiller.

'Move it to the right if you want her to go left, and left to go right,' he said. 'Try it. You'll get the hang of it.'

Lockie tried it and found the boat answering easily to his touch. The water looked black and awesome. He sensed the great depth underneath, full of fish and crabs, and dead sailors, and who knows, maybe sea monsters never seen by human eyes.

The gunwale was not too far from the water and he was scared by the thought of falling overboard. He crouched lower on the seat at the stern.

They soon came to an inlet walled by high rock cliffs. At the far end of the inlet Gerry shipped his oars.

He came to the stern and asked Lockie to swap places with him. Lockie watched him shoot the net. When the last of it had gone overboard, they threw out a red marker buoy.

'Don't bother with the tiller, Lockie,' Gerry said on the way back. 'Would you like to try a line?'

'What's a line?'

Gerry reached under the seat and brought up a square frame with fishing-line wrapped around it, and a number of hooks and coloured feathers attached. He undid the hooks from the line and dropped them over the stern. Then he played out the line for about twenty yards. He threw the frame with the remaining line on the floor of the boat and handed the line to Lockie.

'Now,' he said, 'if you feel a tug, haul it in.'

He resumed his seat and joined the others at the rowing. Lockie sat there holding the line. There was a gentle, steady pull on it as it trailed behind the boat, but not what he would describe as a 'tug'.

The line pulled suddenly at Lockie's fingers. 'A tug!' he said excitedly. 'I think I felt a tug.'

'Haul it in,' said Gerry, and Lockie hauled it in, hand over hand. He forgot his fear of the water and leaned over the side to see if he had caught anything. As he drew in the last couple of fathoms of the line, he saw not one but two silver fish gleaming as they were pulled up through the dark water to the surface.

He raised them out of the water and held the line up for the others to view them. They jiggled on the hooks, their tails flapping as they came into the air.

Lockie just sat there, staring at them. He didn't know how to take them off the hooks, but Gerry came to the rescue and showed him how to ease the hooks off.

'Two nice mackerel,' Jack said.

The mackerel threshed and thumped the floor of the boat with their tails as Lockie let out the hooks again. Before they reached shore, he had ten mackerel. They ran pieces of string through the gills of the fish to bring them home, three each for Gerry and Jack, and four for Lockie and Pasha.

'About four o'clock,' Jack said as they parted.

When they got home, Mammy Tallon was at the door to greet them. 'You've a nice strap of fish there, Lockie,' she said.

They had the fish for lunch. Afterwards Pasha went to the shed and rolled a timber barrel out. He brought it to the tap on the back wall of the house and washed it thoroughly with a scrubbing brush. He left it to dry on the wall at the back of the yard.

'What's that for?' Lockie asked.

'For the fish,' Pasha said.

'We haven't caught any yet,' Lockie said.

'We will.'

Pasha carried a sack as they went back to the strand at four o'clock as arranged. The others were already there, sitting on the ground. They too had sacks. They launched the boat and rowed out again. The water was dead calm, and to Lockie it seemed more sinister than when they ran over a swell in the morning. The surface had been moving then, making the water appear more solid.

Gerry hauled the net and the catch was good, pollock, mainly, a few cod and herring, quite a few mackerel, and just one bream. One fish came up that looked like a small shark, its open mouth underneath its body showing sharp teeth.

'Aha, you scamp!' Jack said viciously when he saw it.

'What is it?' Lockie asked.

'A dogfish,' Gerry said as he hammered its head on the gunwale with the tiller. When the fish was limp, he extricated it from the net and threw it overboard.

'Why don't you keep it?' Lockie asked.

'Nobody eats dog fish,' Gerry said. 'Fishermen hate them. They're scavengers. They prey on fish caught in the net.'

When they got home, Pasha put the sack of fish on the ground beside a heavy table near the tap in the yard. He gutted the fish and washed them.

Mammy Tallon put a bed of salt in the barrel, and, as each fish was cleaned, she laid it on the bed of salt. Every layer of fish was covered with a layer of salt until the barrel was nearly full, but three large pollock were put aside.

'Three for tomorrow,' Mammy Tallon said.

Pasha threw the offal in the field at the other side of the yard wall, and before they had gone into the house, a flock of seagulls came screaming to gobble it up.

CHAPTER TWENTY-ONE

A New School

Lockie settled quickly into his island world. Every day there was something new to experience, a fresh discovery. In many of its ways the island was like a place that had gone back in time, especially in Pasha and Mammy Tallon's house.

He shared the work of the house and fields with them. They were poor, even by the standards that he had known in his foster homes. But they were not hungry. There was always enough to eat.

Breakfast was porridge, tea and bread and butter. For lunch they had fish and potatoes and some kind of vegetable taken from Pasha's garden at the south side of the house, cabbage, turnips, carrots, parsnips. They had their last meal at about seven o'clock, which was eggs and bread baked by Mammy Tallon.

In the press under the dresser there was a flour bin and bags of oatmeal, bread soda, sugar and rice. They had a rice pudding on Sundays. Pasha and Mammy Tallon were very old-fashioned.

'What's all this craze for new things?' Pasha asked once.

'People aren't content with enough any more. They're listening to ads on the radio and watching them on TV day in, day out, coaxing them to buy bigger, better, and faster gadgets to make their lives easy. They'll soon forget what they have hands and legs for.'

Mammy Tallon agreed: 'Once you have health and a bite to eat, aren't you all right?'

Gradually Lockie lost his fear of being sent back to the Farrells. He went often to the village on errands for Pasha or Mammy Tallon. He went across the fields, over the hill, a distance of about a half a mile. To go along the road which circled the island would be a journey of two miles.

The first time he went to the shop he knocked at the door.

'Hello,' the shop lady said when she came to the door. 'You must be Lockie.' She smiled broadly at him and shook his hand. 'What are you knocking for? Why don't you just walk in?

It was not a real shop, like the ones Lockie knew, just a house like Mammy Tallon's with the goods for sale on the shelves of the dresser. They sold matches, cigarettes, tobacco, sugar, tea, salt and pepper for the table, and other odds and ends. Mrs O'Neill, the shop lady, gave him a bag of boiled sweets. 'For yourself,' she said.

In a short time he was known to all on the island. He became an islander.

Lockie was there a week when Pasha and Mammy Tallon decided to send him to school. Pasha had spent most of the previous evening making a school bag for him out of a piece of an old sail. It had a strap to go across his shoulder. Mammy Tallon put a few slices of bread and butter in the bag and accompanied him to the school.

They knocked at the door and a boy opened it. He was about Lockie's age, blond hair and bright blue eyes. When he saw them, he turned towards the top of the classroom.

'It's Lockie, Miss Doolan,' he said, and he returned to his place.

From the doorway Lockie could see one long desk. The boy who opened the door sat there alone. The rest of the room was out of sight behind the open door. Miss Doolan was dark with a touch of grey in her hair. She wore glasses, and there was a soft look about her face that Lockie liked at once.

'Lockie's welcome, Mrs Underwood,' she said to Mammy Tallon. Hearing her called that was strange.

'Lockie, sit beside Pat O'Hare,' Miss Doolan said, and the boy who had opened the door for them smiled at him and moved in to make room on the seat. Lockie went in and sat beside Pat while Mammy Tallon and Miss Doolan spoke at the door.

The room was long, like schoolrooms everywhere. There were six long desks in all, of three different sizes. The two at the back were the highest and the two at the front were quite low. There were fifteen children in the room, from the four little children in the front desk to the two oldest children, Pat and Lockie, at the back.

The teacher returned to the top of the room and welcomed Lockie again.

'This is Loughlin Underwood,' she told the other children. She may have called him by his correct name, but already the islanders had named him 'Lockie Pasha', and that name would always be his on the island.

She opened a cupboard and took out a few books, including three exercise books, and gave them to Lockie.

'Pat, show him your assignment,' she said, and Pat showed Lockie the page and the problems to be solved in their maths book. In the meantime Miss Doolan crouched down before the small desks at the front and took to showing the children there how to make letters.

'I live on the same side of the island as you,' Pat whispered.

'Where?'

'Do you know the two houses down from Pasha's?'

'Yes.' They were the only houses other than Pasha's on that side of the island. Lockie had never been near them. His wanderings had always taken him across the hill towards the village, never in the direction of those other houses.

'Well, I live in the one nearest to yours.'

'Do you come across the hill to school?' Lockie asked.

'I do. We'll be home together to the top of the hill.'

'Right.'

Lockie had little trouble with the maths assignments. He had little trouble with any of the school subjects. Pat soon came to rely on him to explain things to him. They conversed in whispers. Miss Doolan encouraged it as long as they didn't interfere with the work of the other children.

They were allowed to move about the classroom, to consult the encyclopedia, the dictionary, or any other book on the bookshelves at the end of the room, to pare a pencil into the wastepaper basket. Lockie had never known a schoolroom so free.

With Lockie and Pat, Miss Doolan rarely used the blackboard. She came down to them when the other children were working quietly at some assignment and said, 'Let me in the middle, Lockie.'

Then she sat between the two boys and worked on a sheet

of paper to demonstrate a maths procedure, or whatever needed explanation.

It was a happy school, and Lockie looked forward to going there every morning. If Miss Doolan was partly the reason for that, so was Pat O'Hare. Other than Mickey Wheeler he had never had a closer friend.

The days went by quickly. Lockie was busy about the house and yard and in the fields. He brought in the turf from the stack that stood at the side of the yard, he fed the hens, drove the cow to the stream to drink, took her to the yard to be milked, fed her hay when she was brought in to the shed at night, cleaned out the shed, learned to milk her.

Pasha or Mammy Tallon went to the mainland once every month, to Skeheen where they got supplies of flour, salt for preserving fish, oil for lamps, and occasionally batteries for the radio. They always brought Lockie something, a packet of sweets and something for school, a pencil or coloured crayons.

On some afternoons and on weekends Pasha brought Lockie rod-fishing. He made a rod for him, a long pole with a series of heavy staples to thread the line through. They went to various places on the rocks on the foreshore, and Pasha showed Lockie how to find crabs and limpets for bait by turning over stones in rock pools, and how to tie the bait on the hooks. Always they caught fish. Pasha had a magic touch. He seemed to know when and where the fish were likely to bite and which bait to use, and Lockie was quick to learn.

Best of all, Pasha taught Lockie how to ride the motor-bike. Sometimes after school he rode it to the south end of the island. The road was bumpy, and the bike, even when flat out, had no great speed, but Lockie didn't mind that.

He loved the feel of its power as it throbbed under him and the wind on his face was exhilarating.

Lockie thought he knew everything there was to know about the island then, but one day Pat said, 'Would you like to see my secret place?'

'What? You have a secret place?'

'Yes. Would like to see it?'

'Of course I would! Where is it?'

'Meet me after school and I'll show you. Don't tell Pasha or Mammy Tallon about it. It's my secret.'

They met at the top of the hill after school. They went down to the village and headed south along the road towards the cliffs. Lockie followed Pat across a field, bare except for a few yellow ragwort plants. They clambered over the stone fence at the end of the field and across a short grassy margin to the edge of the cliff.

Pat walked to the edge and looked down without a trace of nervousness. Lockie stood a few yards back from the edge and gazed down at the moving water a hundred and fifty feet below. He stepped back as he felt a giddiness in his head.

His heart jumped as Pat stepped forward and vanished out of sight over the edge. Without thinking of the awesome drop to the sea, he rushed forward and looked down. Pat stood smiling on a wide ledge about six feet below the clifftop.

'Come on down,' he said.

'I'm not going to jump,' Lockie said as the feeling of giddiness came back.

He turned around looking back to land. He knelt down, then lay flat, face down, and moved slowly backward until his legs were over the edge. Slowly he lowered himself until only his arms held him to the clifftop. He grasped tufts of the rough seaside grass and stayed there afraid to let go. He had lost confidence, imagining that the ledge had vanished and there was nothing beneath him but the long drop to the water.

'It's all right. Just drop down. The ledge is very wide,' Pat reassured him.

He closed his eyes and let go. When his feet struck the ledge, he toppled backward and screamed. Pat laughed as Lockie fell to a sitting position on the solid ledge. He sat there for a while, trying to overcome his fear of the high cliff.

The ledge was about ten feet wide and stretched for about fifty yards along the face of the cliff. Pat went to an opening in the rock wall close by and went in. Lockie, still afraid to stand up, crawled on hands and knees and followed. It was a cave, not very deep and with a roof high enough to allow the boys to stand up. It was bone dry.

Pat sat on a heap of hay on the floor and opened a timber box. Lockie sat beside him. The box contained two apples, yellow and wrinkled, a book called *Wonders of the Physical World*, four pieces of candle, a box of matches, a ball of string, a magnifying glass, and a small mirror.

'Are those things yours?' Lockie asked.

'They are,' said Pat. 'Who else would put them here. Didn't I tell you this was a secret place? Nobody knows about it but me.'

'What do you want the candles for?'

'In case I have to come here at night.'

'Why would you come here at night?'

'If the island was invaded by pirates or something. I'd have a place to escape.'

'Oh!'

They ate the two apples and stayed at the mouth of the

cave for a half-hour or more, looking at the gently moving sea and the sun dropping towards the horizon. When the sky was reddening low down to the west they scrambled up to the clifftop and went home.

Lockie swore that he would not tell anyone about the cave.

CHAPTER TWENTY-TWO

Christmas on the Island

Dadge arrived three days before Christmas. He left the jennet at Mike Donovan's and took the ferry into the south end of the island. They rushed to greet the wanderer when he set foot inside the door.

He spent the night by the fire telling them about his travels, and he didn't mind bending the truth if it made a better story. It was late when they got to bed, and the talking didn't stop then, for Dadge and Lockie whispered across the space between the beds long into the night.

Lockie felt a little uneasy going to sleep because Dadge's presence reminded him of the flight from Cloughlee and the danger of being found again and returned to the Farrells.

The day before Christmas Eve, Lockie and Mammy Tallon went across to the mainland to do 'a bit of Christmas shopping', as Pasha called it. They went on Harrington's ferry from the south side of the island. Lockie was reluctant to go at first, but Pasha assured him that no one in Skeheen would know who he was or be interested in him in any way.

The town of Skeheen was thronged with people. Cars

crawled like snails in a continuous line through the main streets. The noise of car engines and people shouting to make themselves heard above the din of traffic made Lockie dizzy. He had grown so used to the quiet of the island.

The footpaths were crowded, people hurrying or dawdling, talking, greeting, many of them laden with shopping bags full of Christmas fare. Two buskers playing banjo and accordion at a street corner were doing a roaring trade. It was a cheerful bustle, and when Lockie grew accustomed to it, he began to enjoy the noise and the movement.

The manager of the supermarket and the people at the check-out knew Mammy Tallon and greeted her like a long-lost friend. They offered to hold her purchases until she was ready to take the ferry back to the island.

Lockie went with her to a clothes shop. They had to go to the back of the shop to the boys' department. Mammy Tallon bought a zip-up green jacket for Lockie, with four pockets on the outside and two in the heavy lining.

'That's for the cold weather in January and February,' Mammy Tallon said. 'You can wear it now if you like.'

She bought a cap for Pasha and a pair of thick woollen socks for Dadge.

'What are you getting for yourself?' Lockie asked her.

'I have enough. I don't want for anything.'

'But it's Christmas.'

'Christmas or any other time, I have all I want.'

'Do you mind if I walk around the town by myself for a while?'

'All right, but be sure to be at the pier for the ferry at half past three at the latest.'

Lockie had twelve pounds in his shirt pocket. It was the money they gave him at the funfair in Kiltarr when he was leaving for Cloughlee. He had never had an opportunity to spend it.

He went first to a jeweller's shop, but he hadn't enough for the things he wanted to buy for Mammy Tallon. The lady in the shop asked him how much he was thinking of spending on the present for his mother.

'About twelve pounds.'

'Oh, we wouldn't have anything here in that range. Have you thought of a box of chocolates, or lace handkerchiefs, or a little ornament for the mantelpiece?'

'I hadn't, but thanks for the idea.'

He went to a shop selling newspapers, and books and souvenirs. He wandered around, looking at the merchandise. There was so much that he found it hard to make a choice. A lady came to him.

'Can I help you, boy?'

'Well, I'm just trying to get something for my mother for Christmas.'

'And how much do you want to spend on your mother?'

'About ten or twelve pounds.'

'Which is it, ten or twelve?'

'Ten. I want to keep some.'

He didn't like any of the things she showed him, so he went back to the clothes shop. The woman there helped him to choose a present for Mammy Tallon, a shawl, black with red and gold patterns around the edge. It cost seven pounds fifty, so he had four-fifty left to get something for Pasha and Dadge.

The shop lady wrapped the shawl for him in fancy paper and gave him a card to put in with it. He wrote on the card: *To Mammy Tallon for Christmas, with love and thanks from Lockie.*

For Pasha he got two spinners in a fish tackle shop. They put them in a white cardboard box and tied it with red twine. Lockie printed on the cover: *To Pasha from Lockie.*

In a hardware shop he found plastic boxes of different sizes and he bought four of them for Dadge – one for tea, one for sugar, one for butter, and one for salt.

When they got home from Skeheen, Pasha and Dadge had decorated the house with holly. They had killed and cleaned two hens that Mammy Tallon had been fattening for the Christmas dinner. The hens were hanging near the back door. They had cut the sides of two turnips to make flat surfaces, and gouged holes in them to hold the Christmas candles.

On Christmas Eve Mammy Tallon made stuffing for the hens with breadcrumbs, onions and sage and thyme. In the evening they had tea and afterwards they opened their presents. Lockie got the green jacket. They had wrapped it again when they got home from Skeheen the day before. Pasha gave him a penknife, and Dadge gave him apples in a small plastic bag.

Mammy Tallon gave the others their new socks and cap.

'Waste of money!' she said when she saw the shawl, but she smiled as she threw it across her shoulders and walked up and down for them to admire.

'Thank you, Lockie,' she said. 'That will look nice when I wear it to town.'

After the presents they lit the Christmas candles. The candles, in their turnip candlesticks, were placed on the table. Dadge removed his cap.

'You light them,' Mammy Tallon said to Lockie, and she gave him a box of matches. 'It's always the youngest who lights the candles.'

Lockie struck a match and lit them.

'*Go mbeirimid beo ag an am seo arís,*' Dadge said solemnly.

'What's that?' Lockie asked.

'A prayer in Irish,' Mammy Tallon told him. 'It's a wish that we might all be alive to enjoy Christmas again next year.'

She put the candles in the windows.

'Why do you put them there?' Lockie asked.

'You remember the Christmas story. There was no room at the inn for Mary and Joseph. We put the candles in the window to let them know that they'd be welcome in this house if they came this way.'

Later all four of them went across the field behind the house to the top of the hill. It was a cloudless night with a starry sky. When the light of the kitchen had faded from their eyes, they could see their way easily enough.

The view from the top of the hill was magnificent. Candle flame glowed brightly in every window of the island houses, and in the houses in islands near by, and faintly in the distance in the houses on the mainland.

Christmas Day was quiet. Pasha and Dadge wandered along the shore in the morning. When dinner was ready, Lockie went to find them. He saw them by the water's edge, Pasha standing still, looking out to sea, and Dadge gesticulating excitedly as he spoke.

Three days after Christmas Dadge left. Mammy Tallon wanted him to stay until the fine weather came, but he insisted on going.

'I'm too long here already. I'm like a cat on a hot griddle if I'm more than two days in the one place.'

'But the nights will be cold up the country in January and February,' she reminded him.

'Not so cold that a good fire and plenty of clothes on me won't keep it out of the old bones.'

Pasha and Lockie brought him out to the strand below Mike Donovan's. They stayed until he had tackled the jennet and moved away at a canter on the road to Skeheen.

CHAPTER TWENTY-THREE

Looking to the Future

Spring slipped into early summer, and Lockie was happy. He had settled into life on the island as if he had been born there. Pasha and Mammy Tallon treated him with a kindness he had never known. He got used to them, to their strange ways, and to their frugal way of life.

Always at the back of his mind there was the fear that it was too good to last. He was still afraid that '*they*', whoever they might be, would find him and return him to the Farrell home in Cloughlee or to some family that he hated, and he would be plunged into misery again.

One day when school had ended and the pupils were leaving, Miss Doolan called Lockie back.

'Have your parents made plans for next year?' she asked.

'Next year?' Lockie said, and he pretended to be puzzled. He knew very well that she was talking about his moving on to secondary school. Pat O'Hare had told him that he was going to the Community College in Skeheen, but Lockie didn't want to talk about it. He didn't even want to think about it.

'Oh, never mind,' Miss Doolan said. 'Would you tell your

parents that I'd like to call to see them? I'll be over this evening some time after tea.'

When Lockie told them, Mammy Tallon jumped up at once and began to tidy the kitchen, stowing old newspapers under the chair cushions, re-arranging cups and plates on the dresser, sweeping the floor. To Lockie it made little difference to the appearance of the place; as far as he was concerned it was always spotless.

'Lockie's teacher is coming to see us, Pasha,' she said.

'Easy, there now,' Pasha said. 'Lockie hasn't done anything wrong. Have you, Lockie?'

'No! Nothing!'

But Mammy Tallon wasn't reassured. She fussed about all evening, moving in and out, upstairs and down.

When Miss Doolan arrived, she said. 'I was wondering what you intend to do with Lockie next year. He'll have finished the primary cycle and should be going on to secondary school.'

'There's no secondary school on this island,' Mammy Tallon said.

'I know. That's why I think it's time to make plans for his future.'

Pasha and Mammy Tallon were silent.

'He's a highly intelligent boy,' Miss Doolan said, 'one of the best I've ever had in my school. It would be a pity if he didn't continue his education. I expect he'll have a bright future in whatever he decides to do.'

'But what can we do about it when there's no secondary school on the island?' Pasha asked.

'Would it be possible to send him out to town, to stay with a family there during the week and return to the island on weekends when the crossing is safe?'

'No!' Mammy Tallon said vehemently. 'It would not be possible.'

'It's just one of the options that occurred to me,' Miss Doolan said.

'What are the other options?' Pasha asked.

'There aren't many others really. Next year he could remain in the school here, but he would be on his own in seventh class. Pat O'Hare is going to town to attend the Community College there.'

'He could stay in your school, then?'

'Yes, of course. I'd be delighted to have him back, but it's only putting off the day when he must go to the mainland for further schooling.'

'I don't want further schooling,' Lockie said quietly. 'I want to stay on the island.'

'He'll stay on the island,' Mammy Tallon said, and she rose to put on the kettle. 'You'll have a cup of tea, Miss Doolan?'

'No. No, thank you. I must be going. I thought I'd better mention this to you. I hope you don't mind.'

'No. It's very kind of you to take such an interest in Lockie,' Pasha said. 'He can stay with you for another year anyway. We'll have time to think about it in the meanwhile.'

When Miss Doolan had gone, Lockie asked Pasha what he meant by saying they would think about it.

'There is nothing to think about. I'm staying on the island for ever and ever. You know what will happen if I go out there. They'll send me back to Cloughlee.'

'Maybe in a year's time you'll be forgotten on the mainland,' Pasha said. 'Who would be interested in putting you away? They don't care about you out there. They don't care about poor people like us. They don't want to know you exist.'

'Would you have to pay for me to stay with someone on the mainland while I was going to school?'

'We would.'

'Then that's it!' Lockie said forcefully. 'End of story. Where would you get money to pay for me out there? I'm not going.'

He thought for a little while. 'That's if you don't want to get rid of me,' he added.

'You know very well we don't want to be rid of you,' said Mammy Tallon.

'Yes, I know that.'

They talked about it until bed-time but came to no decision. Lockie could not sleep that night. The future seemed threatening again. Ridiculous solutions flowed into his mind, like stowing away on a boat to Argentina, and joining the street kids in Buenos Aires. Miss Doolan told them about that when they were studying South America.

Mammy Tallon and Pasha talked through the night. The murmur of their voices came to him, and they went on and on. They were still talking when tiredness overcame him and he dropped into a shallow sleep, troubled by the menace of his forebodings.

〰   〰   〰

When he awoke in the morning, he thought he had been asleep for no more than a few minutes. The voices were still droning in his ears. But he felt the brightness of day on his eyelids and he sat up in bed. Pasha and Mammy Tallon were still talking, but now their voices came from downstairs.

Mammy Tallon was busy about the kitchen when Lockie came down. Pasha had gone out to bring in some turf for the

149

fire. She was more cheerful than she had been the night before.

'Good morning, Lockie,' she said. 'How are you feeling?'

There was that musical note of merriment in her voice that Lockie noticed when she was joyful.

'What's going on?' Lockie asked.

Pasha came in with a basket of turf before Mammy Tallon could answer.

'There's nothing going on,' she said. 'We've made up our minds. That's all. Tell him, Pasha.'

'We have so,' Pasha responded.

'What have you made up your minds about?' Lockie asked.

'We're sending you to school. Tell him, Pasha.'

'You'll be starting in Skeheen in September,' Pasha said simply.

Pasha stoked the fire. Mammy Tallon poured tea for Lockie, then fussed about, touching a curtain to ensure that it hung straight, moving a chair, re-arranging cups on the dresser, her hands fluttering nervously.

'How?' Lockie asked.

'How what?' Pasha said.

'How are you going to pay for my education this morning when it was impossible last night.'

'You're a most inquisitive young fellow,' Mammy Tallon rebuked him. 'Don't worry your head about that. Pasha and I have found a way. Just leave it to us.'

'I won't go. How do I know what you're doing to send me to school?'

'Does it matter?' Pasha asked him.

'Yes.'

'Well, we can't tell you just yet. It has to be our secret for the present. Okay?'

Lockie thought for a minute. 'All right,' he said eventually. 'If you're not going to tell me, there's nothing I can do about it. But remember, I don't want to go at all, money or no money. I want to stay here on the island.'

'The island and this house will always be a home for you,' Pasha said. 'School is only for a while, and anyway, you'll be home every weekend.'

The decision had been made, and Lockie felt helpless. He talked about it with his friend at school. Pat was delighted at the prospect of their being in secondary school together.

And as time went by Lockie came to accept the decision, although the fear of being found out and sent back to the Farrells nagged at him like a chronic toothache.

CHAPTER TWENTY-FOUR

The New Man

It was June, the last days in school before the summer holidays. For Lockie and Pat O'Hare it was their last days in the island school. They had lost all enthusiasm for study, and Miss Doolan gave them odd cleaning and tidying work, organising and cataloguing the books in the school library, putting her own papers in order. Other times she sent them on errands around the island.

It was also the time of tourists. A few houses kept guests, just one or two in each house, except for 'Ocean View'. That was a large house, and the Harringtons, Jim and Maura, catered for a full house of tourists during the months of June, July and August, as well as a few stragglers through September and October.

Pat and Lockie were engaged to help in the kitchen and garden, to guide the tourists around the island, especially to help those who wanted to fish with rods from the rocks on the foreshore. Lockie knew all the best spots. The Harringtons were delighted with him.

One evening in mid-July, well past nine o'clock, Pat and Lockie were going home along the road, past a summer bungalow owned by a Dublin family, the Dempseys. They came to stay there every year for the first two weeks in August. During the rest of the summer it was rented to various people. A light was showing in one of the rooms.

'Dempseys' is let,' Lockie said, when he got home.

'Yes, I heard,' Mammy Tallon said.

'Is it a family?' Lockie asked.

'No. A new man. A man on his own, I believe. They tell me he's from the Midlands somewhere.'

'Out for a bit of fishing, I'm told,' Pasha said. 'You might get a job with him.'

〰   〰   〰

The following morning Lockie was up early as usual and on his way to the Harringtons by seven o'clock. It was a fine morning, blue sky and calm sea, just a slight nip in the air before the sun got up to drive away the night chill.

Pat came out to join him as he passed the O'Hare house. Together they walked along the road towards 'Ocean View'.

'There's the new man,' Pat said.

The new man in Dempseys' was already up, standing on the little height at the side of the bungalow, looking around him at sea and land. No doubt he saw the two boys on the road and, as they drew near, he came down the short gravelled drive to greet them.

He was a thick-set man, red-faced, greying hair. But his most peculiar feature was a deep scar from his right eye to his mouth. He was dressed in casual clothes, jeans, a check shirt, and a red jumper.

'Good morning, boys,' the new man greeted them with a broad smile.

Pat answered for both of them, 'Good morning, sir.'

'Where are you off to so early in the morning?'

'We're going to work, sir,' Pat said. Lockie remained silent. Hadn't he seen that man and heard that voice before?

'Aren't you young to be working? Where do you work? Tell me.'

'At "Ocean View", sir. We do jobs for the Harringtons when the visitors are here.'

'Ah, isn't that grand! And what about this little man here? Have you nothing to say for yourself, young man?'

'No, sir,' said Lockie softly.

'Now tell me this, boys. Is there anyone around here who could show me where I could do a bit of fishing? Off the rocks that is. Just to catch one or two for my own frying pan.'

Lockie remembered. The new man was the priest from Cloughlee who had been at the funfair in Kiltarr the day they decided to send him back to the Farrells. It was difficult to be sure that it was the same man, because without his clerical collar and black hat, he looked different. But there was that scar beside his nose. Those features were burned into Lockie's memory, and he felt again the sinking feeling he had on that awful day when they decided to send him back.

Before Pat could say a word, Lockie said, 'I'm Joe Doyle, sir, and this is Pat O'Hare. Pat could be your guide. He knows all the island.'

Pat was dumbstruck. Lockie was the one who knew all the good fishing spots. He guessed that Lockie had some reason for pretending he was someone else, so he didn't give the game away.

'I wouldn't mind, sir. But don't listen to Lo—Joe there. There are others on the island who know where all the good spots are, much better than I do.'

154

'I think you're being modest now. Could you give me a hand this afternoon, say about two-thirty?'

'You'd have to ask Mr Harrington, sir. I don't know if he could spare me.'

'Oh, that's all right. I'll drop down there this morning and ask him. Good morning to ye now.'

He turned to go back to the house, but paused and looked at Lockie. 'Did we meet before, Joe?' he asked.

'No, sir. I don't think so. Were you here last year?'

'No, no,' the priest muttered as he turned and walked away. 'Must be mixing you up with someone else.'

Lockie found it hard to concentrate during the day. He was uneasy. Maybe the priest didn't recognise him at once, but he might remember at any time. Maura Harrington had to speak to him a few times to call him back to reality from his daydreams.

He ran home the long way, by the back road to the school and then over the hill. Mammy Tallon was surprised when she looked out the kitchen window and saw him coming across the field towards the back door.

'Do you know who has Dempseys'?' he asked when he went in. Pasha was sitting by the front window, setting a saw.

'I feel you're going to tell me,' he said.

'The priest.'

'What priest?'

'The one that wanted to send me back to Cloughlee that day at the funfair.'

Pasha stopped and looked out the window. Mammy Tallon turned from the back door and stood staring at Lockie.

'What, what–' Mammy Tallon began to say something, then stopped, her hands moving as if she were trying to mould shapes in the air in front of her.

'Are you sure?' Pasha asked.

'Dead sure.'

'Did he know you?'

'I don't know. I told him my name was Joe Doyle. He said he thought he saw me before but couldn't remember.'

Pasha thought for a moment. 'He was lying,' he said quietly.

'Oh no, Pasha,' Mammy Tallon said, agitated. 'Surely be to the Lord God he didn't remember. It's a long time now. Too long for him to remember. Surely. Surely!'

'Not to remember Lockie, Mammy Tallon? Not to remember a boy with a strong face like our Lockie's? I believe the priest was lying. He remembers all right.'

'What – what to do now, Pasha? What are we going to do?'

'Nothing,' Pasha said quietly. 'We must wait and see what the priest does about it. We have no more places to hide.'

'What do I do while we're waiting?' Lockie asked.

'Nothing. Just wait.'

CHAPTER TWENTY-FIVE

This is Home

Lockie went back to work the next day. The new man had seen him, and there was no point in hiding. Wherever he went on the island people greeted him cheerfully and conspiratorially as 'Joe Doyle'. The island was a small place and the people in it were like members of a single family.

Pasha was again proven to be right. The priest did remember Lockie. It was almost a fortnight after he had met him on the road on the way to work – the priest's last day on the island – that the ferry brought Miss Cuneen among its passengers.

Jim Harrington owned the only car on the island, an old banger, a Ford Capri. Miss Cuneen hired him to drive her to Pasha's house.

'I'll be busy for about an hour,' he told her. 'Would you like to sit in the visitors' lounge, and I'll get the girls to bring you a cup of tea while you're waiting.'

He told Lockie to peep through the service hatch to see if he knew the woman. Lockie recognised her right away and told him who she was. Jim sent him home with the news of her arrival.

'Did you see her?' Pasha asked.

'I saw her.'

Mammy Tallon couldn't speak for a minute. 'What will we do now?' she said eventually.

'What can we do?' Pasha said. 'She's here, and she knows we're here. Our priest friend has a busy mouth it seems.'

'I think she's okay,' Lockie said. 'I don't think she wanted to send me back to the Farrells.'

The sound of Jim Harrington's Capri cut short their conversation. Its exhaust was shattered, and whenever it started up, it could be heard all over the island. People would turn to each other and say, 'I wonder where Jim is off to now?'

Mammy Tallon smoothed back her hair and sat on the armchair by the fire. Pasha went to the front gate to greet the newcomer.

'A visitor for you, Pasha,' Jim Harrington said when he pulled up at the gate. 'Miss Cuneen from Dublin.'

'I know Miss Cuneen. We met before.'

Miss Cuneen smiled and gave Pasha her hand. Lockie watched them through the window. Miss Cuneen wore a suit as usual, but this one was pale green. Pasha showed her in.

'Afternoon, Mammy Tallon,' she said and shook hands with her.

'He's not leaving here,' Mammy Tallon said, uttering no word of greeting.

Miss Cuneen did not respond, but turned to Lockie at the window.

'Hello, Lockie. We've caught up with you at last!'

'Hello, Miss Cuneen.'

'How are you?'

'This is different, Miss Cuneen. This is home.'

'I see. You are happy here then?'

'He's not leaving,' Mammy Tallon repeated.

'That's not my decision to make. I was sent to make out a report on his present circumstances. That's all.'

'Who sent you?' Pasha asked.

'The Eastern Health Board. Although Lockie is now in the Southern Board's area, he is still on our files.'

'Why the sudden interest in him now?'

'Well, I don't know if I should tell you this, but Father James Shanahan of Cloughlee phoned the Director saying he knew of his present whereabouts and that he was concerned for his welfare.'

'Why is he concerned?'

'I don't know. All I know is I have to report on Lockie's present circumstances and the Board will then decide on what action, if any, should be taken.'

'What are you going to say in your report?' Pasha continued.

'I'll tell them what I see, no more and no less.'

'All right then. What do you want to know?'

'Everything really. Does he attend school regularly, for example?'

'He hasn't missed a single day since he started in the island school,' Mammy Tallon intervened proudly. 'Next year he'll be going to the Community College in Skeheen.'

Miss Cuneen turned to Pasha. 'Tell me,' she said, and Lockie knew that a key question was coming by the way she shaped her lips and articulated every syllable. 'What is your means of livelihood? I'm sorry, but I have to ask you these questions.'

Pasha told her he was on the dole, but he grew all his own vegetables, had milk from his cow, and caught the odd fish.

He assured her that they could manage to finance his secondary education.

'What about his behaviour?' Miss Cuneen asked. 'Any of those vicious outbursts of uncontrolled rage that caused so much trouble in the past?'

'No!' Mammy Tallon said. 'We've never seen anything like that since he came to live with us. No one else in the island has either. Ask anyone. Ask Jim Harrington. Ask the school teacher.'

'This is different, Miss Cuneen,' Lockie said again. 'This is really home.'

'I see.'

She asked a few questions about his health, his friends, his hobbies, how he spent his time. Lockie answered her, eager to show that he was living a normal life and that he had become a true Tallon Islander.

Miss Cuneen stood up to leave. Mammy Tallon stood too. They shook hands.

'I believe you're a good lady,' Mammy Tallon said. 'I know you'll tell them the truth. Do you think they'll take him away again?'

'I can't say really.' She must have seen the look of anxiety and worry on Mammy Tallon's face. 'But my report will be favourable,' she said, 'and I'll add a recommendation that it would be in Lockie's best interest to be allowed to remain here in your care.'

'Thank you,' said Pasha. 'You couldn't do more than that.'

Lockie accompanied her to the south-end ferry and stood on the pier waving goodbye to her as it left.

⌇ ⌇ ⌇

Three long weeks went by as they waited for some communication from the Eastern Health Board. When it came, it was not through the post.

Lockie was watching the ferry docking at the south-end pier. One by one the passengers got out. Then Lockie saw something that made his stomach tighten. The priest from Cloughlee, the new man, stepped on to the pier accompanied by a guard in uniform.

Jim Harrington invited them into the house for a cup of coffee. They had three full hours to kill on the island before the next ferry sailed for the mainland. Jim slipped away to warn Lockie.

'They're going to your house,' he said. 'Run home and tell them.'

Lockie burst into the kitchen. 'The guard is here,' he said. 'He came in the ferry, and the priest is with him.'

'What priest?'

'The new man that was in Dempseys'.'

'Oh, my God!' Mammy Tallon exclaimed. 'I thought the Cuneen girl had put an end to all that.'

They spent an anxious half-hour, waiting for the guard to call. Pasha sat like a stone image, not moving. Mammy Tallon was in her butterfly mode, flitting around the house, swiping with a vicious towel at imaginary specks of dust on chairs and table, on the radio and on the shelves of the dresser. Lockie sat by the window, looking down the road in the direction of Dempseys' bungalow.

'They're coming!' he said at last.

'Two of them?' Pasha asked in disbelief.

'Yes.'

'All right. Come away from the window. Sit there near the radio, and don't talk.'

The priest and the guard from Skeheen arrived at the door. Lockie heard their feet crunch on the gravel and cinders leading up to the house from the road. Then there was a pause followed by a gentle rapping on the door.

'Come in, Guard,' Pasha called.

The guard came in, a tall, grey-haired man. Lockie spotted the sergeant's stripes on his sleeve. He was followed by Father Shanahan.

'Oh, it's you, Barney,' Pasha said as he stood up and offered his hand to the sergeant. They shook hands warmly and looked into each other's eyes.

The sergeant turned to Mammy Tallon and shook her hand. 'Good day to you, Mammy Tallon,' he said.

Then he turned to Lockie and shook his hand too. 'So this is the young man I've been hearing about,' he said.

All the time the priest stood silent just inside the kitchen door, completely ignored by the others until the sergeant turned to him and said, 'It's okay now, Father. I'll manage by myself from here.'

'But–' the new man was about to say something, when Pasha interrupted.

'I'd be thankful to you, sir, if you left my house,' he said quietly. When Pasha spoke quietly like that, it had a chilling effect on a person. Like all people who had a quiet way about them, it was impossible to know the depth of his feeling or where exactly his flash-point was.

The new man stood with a wide-eyed stare for a few seconds. His mouth opened like a fish in a jar. Then it closed again. The others looked at him in silence. He turned on his heel and went out the door. They heard him crunch his way to the road.

CHAPTER TWENTY-SIX

Date with Destiny

'Sit down, Barney,' Pasha said. 'Take the load off your feet.'

The sergeant sat down.

'I was just going to make a pot of tea,' Mammy Tallon 'Would you like to join us?'

'If you're making it for yourself, sure I might as well,' the sergeant said.

Mammy Tallon filled the kettle at the sink and put it on the fire. The sergeant put his cap on the floor beside his chair.

'We're having a fine spell of weather,' he said. 'The fishing must be good.'

'Never better,' Pasha told him. 'We have four barrels salted already, enough to take us through the winter, and fresh fish most days. Would you like a few pollock? They were caught only this morning.'

'If they're to spare, I wouldn't mind at all.'

After a pause the sergeant said, 'A good few visitors around. A man from Killarney told me yesterday that it's the best season there for forty years.'

'So I'm told,' Pasha said. 'Jim Harrington's is full for most of the summer so far. But Dempseys' was empty until a few weeks ago.'

Lockie wondered when they were going to talk about him and what the sergeant had come for. But the subject was not mentioned. They talked about football matches, farming, fishing, the government, the cost of living, the condition of the roads, how hard it was to find work, people they knew from long ago, everything but the business in hand.

Lockie could stand it no longer. They were drinking the tea Mammy Tallon had made for them and they were eating buttered slices of 'spotted dog' which she had made the day before.

'What about me?' Lockie asked.

'You go out and bring in some turf for the fire, and be quiet like I told you,' Pasha said.

Lockie did as he was told and sat down again, chastened and silent. The others talked on about this and that. Eventually the sergeant stood up to leave.

'Going so soon?' Mammy Tallon said. 'Sure you've only just arrived. Can't you take it easy for another while?'

'There's nothing I'd like better than to sit here talking to yourself and Pasha, and to the young man there for the rest of the evening, but I told Jim Harrington I'd be at the pier by ten past five at the latest.'

Pasha stood up and faced the sergeant. Lockie felt that now was the time for them to discuss the business the sergeant came for.

'We go back a long way, Pasha,' the sergeant said.

'We do.'

'You know, Pasha, that I'd rather be going to any other house on this island or on the mainland than coming here with my story today.'

'I know that, Barney.'

'You know what I'm here for. Is there any need for me to spell it out?'

'No. What's the charge, kidnapping?'

'No, nothing like that. It's a hearing of an application to have the young fellow sent back to that family he was with.'

'Who's applying?'

'The man that came here with me today.'

'The priest?'

'Yes.'

'But can he do that? He has nothing to do with Lockie.'

'I'm afraid he can. It seems that anybody can bring a child before the court to apply for a care order.'

'When is it fixed for?'

'The fifth of September in Skeheen.'

'I'll be there. Must I have Lockie there too?'

'You must, and it might do no harm if your wife was there as well.'

'All right. We'll be there.'

'Your word is good enough for me.'

The two men shook hands and the sergeant fixed his cap on his head and walked slowly to the door. Lockie was on fire with anger. Pasha and Mammy Tallon were going to let them send him away from the island. He was about to follow the two men, but Mammy Tallon held his arm and put her finger to her lips.

They heard the men talking as they walked down to the road.

'They said I was to bring the young lad away with me,' the sergeant was saying.

'No, Barney. You can't. Time enough to talk about that on the fifth of September.'

'That's what I think too, Pasha.'

'Will it get you into trouble?'

'No. We're allowed a little discretion in cases like this. I'll say it's my considered opinion that the child is better off where he is. Listen to me. My eldest girl is a lawyer. If there's anything she can do – and there'll be no charge – just let me know.'

'Thanks, Barney.'

Lockie and Mammy Tallon stood just inside the door, listening. When Pasha and the sergeant reached the road, the new man was there waiting for them. They heard him ask, 'Where's the boy?'

'He's where he belongs,' the sergeant said and he walked down the road in the direction of the pier.

When Pasha came back, Lockie shouted at him, 'You gave him your word!'

'I did, Lockie, and I'll keep my word.'

'You don't want me here. You only want to get rid of me. Go on, say it. I'm a nuisance, amn't I?'

'Lockie!' Mammy Tallon said.

Pasha didn't speak. He stood there looking at Lockie, and the boy couldn't tell from his face how he was feeling. Lockie rushed out the door. He heard Mammy Tallon calling him back and Pasha's quiet voice saying, 'Let him be.'

Lockie ran through the fields to the top of the hill. He didn't know where to turn. The last time he felt so desperate was the day he took the boat at Cloughlee, not caring where he went as long as it was away from the people who were so callous and indifferent to him.

In the end he came to Pat's secret place. The drop down to the ledge held no fears for him now. He had other things on his mind. He crawled into the cave and burst into tears.

Gradually his anger left him. He thought that he might have been unfair to Pasha, and especially to Mammy Tallon. They didn't give the game away on him. It was that priest fellow. I thought priests were supposed to help people, he thought. Is sending me back to that crazy, dry-land sailor helping?

Later, as the light in the cave was fading, he thought he should be going back to the house, but how could he go back? He had walked out on them. To go back now would be to admit he was wrong. Maybe he was wrong. Maybe they really wanted what was the best for him.

But promising to bring him to court so that they could send him back was not the best now, was it? If they really wanted what was best, they would do something about getting away again, to some place where they wouldn't be found. Not by priests. Not by anyone.

No, he wouldn't go back.

The light faded, and it grew dark. It got colder, and he wrapped his arms around his knees trying to make himself as small as possible to keep heat in his body. As the light died, the sound of the water splashing against the bottom of the cliff seemed to grow louder. There was no other sound except an occasional squawk from a homing sea bird.

He didn't sleep much during the night. When he did drop off, he was woken again by the cold or by a sheep complaining in the field above. Morning came and the sun's warmth stole into the cave. Lockie stretched his stiff limbs and crawled outside into the light and the heat. He sat with his back against the face of the cliff and closed his eyes. In no time at all he was in a sound sleep.

'Poor Lockie!' The deep voice woke him. Pasha was standing on the wide ledge beside him.

'How did you know where to find me?' Lockie asked.

'Your friend, Pat, told us after a lot of persuasion, and when we convinced him you might be in danger.'

Pasha sat down beside Lockie. 'What were you going to do?'

'I don't know. But I wasn't going to let them send me back.'

'They might not send you back.'

'They did before.'

'I know, but things might be different now.'

'What's different now?'

'Well, you have someone to talk for you for one thing.'

'Who?'

'Barney McCarthy's girl. They say she's good. And you heard Barney. There'll be no charge.'

'There's no guarantee she can stop them.'

'I know that, but what else can you do? Run away and keep running for the next four or five years?'

'Anything would be better than going back there.'

'That isn't true. Being an outlaw is hard, hard and lonely. Anyway, it doesn't matter what you do, the authorities are in control. I know we don't always agree with what they do or with the way they run our lives, but that's the way things are. We have to face it. There's nowhere else to hide.'

'You didn't talk like that when we made a getaway from Coonmore.'

'That was different. I thought we could be safe on Tallon Island. We decided to give it a try. If that priest hadn't come here on holidays, we'd have got away with it.'

They were silent for a while, gazing out to sea.

'I don't want to go back there, Pasha,' Lockie said sadly.

'I know, and we don't want you to go back either. But we have to let them make that decision. Only then will they let you alone. We'll fight it as well as we can.'

They sat there for an hour, talking and not talking, thinking.

Then Pasha rose to his feet. 'Come on, Lockie. We'll solve nothing here. Let's go home. We have until the fifth of September to think about it.'

When they got to the house, Mammy Tallon scolded Lockie. 'Don't ever do that again, Lockie. I didn't sleep a wink last night worrying about you.'

Lockie continued to work at 'Ocean View' through the summer. Mary McCarthy, the lawyer, came to the island and spent most of one Sunday talking to them about the court hearing. Lockie thought she was very young to be a lawyer, dark and good-looking.

She asked many questions and, when Lockie had finished talking to her, she knew everything about his life in the Farrell home and before that. She asked about every detail. She wanted to know things like how many boys were in the fight in the school yard in Cloughlee, and how many punches Lockie had taken.

'I didn't count,' Lockie told her, 'but it was a lot. Mickey might know. He took a lot too.'

CHAPTER TWENTY-SEVEN

Before the Court

On Monday the third of September the Community College in Skeheen re-opened after the summer vacation. Pasha had arranged for Lockie to board with a Mrs Dooley in Dean O'Brien Street. Several times Lockie had asked Pasha and Mammy Tallon how they were going to pay for his accommodation in the town, but they turned his questions aside, saying, 'She isn't asking for much,' or 'It won't put us back much at all.'

The school followed its normal routine on Tuesday, and Lockie and Pat settled in easily. But Lockie was so anxious about the court on the Wednesday that he was almost unconscious of what was going on around him.

In the afternoon, as he left the classroom, the teacher called him aside and said, 'Good luck tomorrow!'

'What did he say?' Pat asked on the way home.

'He wished me luck for tomorrow. I didn't know they knew about it.'

'Everyone knows about it. Most of the people on the island are coming over for the hearing.'

The night was wet. Lockie lay sleepless in his bed at the

front of the house, listening to sheets of rain being thrown by the wind against the window, and at intervals a car swishing by on the street outside. He lay wondering would he do a runner before morning. Where could he go? Maybe he could find the Wheelers and live with them in their caravan. Maybe he could find Dadge and travel around the country with him on the cart.

Pasha came to collect Lockie at about nine o'clock. Lockie had been ready for a while and waiting anxiously. Mrs Dooley wished him luck as he left the house, sprinkling him with holy water to reinforce her good wishes.

Mammy Tallon was waiting for them in the waiting-room, a large room with plain yellow walls and a line of seats from the door to the back wall. There was no other furniture in the room, no pictures on the wall, nothing.

Mammy Tallon was surrounded by a group of people from the island, all of whom Lockie knew. The Farrells were there too, and Father Shanahan, and Mr Bradley, the teacher from Cloughlee. Tom and Mickey Wheeler stood at the back beside Dadge. Miss Cuneen sat in a chair by the window.

'How did everybody know?' Lockie asked.

'Word must have got around,' Pasha said with a hint of a smile on his lips.

Sergeant McCarthy came in.

'The judge is ready,' he announced. 'All interested parties can go to the room now. It's not in the main courtroom, but in the room to the right of the corridor where all the family law cases are dealt with.'

Everybody trooped into the room. The judge arrived, a tall man with a bushy head of hair, like a lion's mane and the brightest, most piercing eyes that Lockie had ever seen. He cleared the room at once of everyone but the main parties involved. The others were ordered to the waiting-room.

In addition to Lockie, Pasha, Mammy Tallon, and the lawyers, he allowed Miss Cuneen and Father Shanahan to remain. The priest had to be there because he was the one making the application.

The judge put on a pair of gold-rimmed glasses and read from a file handed to him by the clerk. Eventually he put down the paper and removed his glasses.

'Well now, Mr Cleeve,' he said, addressing Father Shanahan's lawyer. 'What are the grounds for this application to have the boy returned to a foster home in Cloughlee?'

'In the first place, Your Worship, he is a child needing special care because of severe personality problems and the Eastern Health Board have placed him in the care of a family capable of dealing effectively with those problems.'

The judge looked at Lockie. 'Anything else?'

'At the moment he is a child not having any home or settled place of abode, or visible means of subsistence–'

'Excuse me,' the judge said, 'but isn't he with these people here, the–' and he looked at his notes, 'Underwoods?'

'He is, Your Worship, but they have custody of him illegally, and our contention is that they are not fit persons for the care of children.'

The judge looked at Lockie and Pasha and Mammy Tallon and asked, 'Why do you describe him as homeless, then?'

'Not homeless in the strict sense of the word "homeless", Your Worship.'

'Well then, tell me about it in the less strict sense, Mr Cleeve.'

'This unfortunate orphan–' Mr Cleeve began, but the judge interrupted. He looked over his glasses when he spoke to people, piercing them with his dagger-grey eyes.

'His fortune, good or otherwise, has nothing to do with it. Please spare me the emotion. He may be unfortunate, and he may even be an orphan, but for the moment let us disregard his fortune.'

Lockie felt that the judge didn't like Mr Cleeve.

'Of course, Your Worship. Please forgive me,' Father Shanahan's lawyer apologised.

'This boy, whom we shall call Loughlin Underwood–'

'What's his real name?' the judge asked.

'It is not known, Your Worship. He was a foundling, left outside a hospital in Galway when about eighteen months old.'

'I see,' the judge said and he looked over his glasses at Lockie. He lowered his eyes and jotted something in his notebook.

'Loughlin has been in five foster homes in the thirteen years of his life.'

'Why has he been in so many places?'

'Unfortunately, Your Worship–'

'Here we go again!'

'Sorry, Your Worship. In all of his foster homes his foster parents found him to be bad-tempered, unruly, and largely unmanageable.'

The judge looked over his glasses at Lockie again, and Lockie thought he saw a faint hint of a smile on his face.

'By the holy, Loughlin,' he said, 'you must be a terror.'

'I–I was, sir,' Lockie said.

'Was, Loughlin? Was? Have you reformed then? Are you not still the wild man of Tallon Island?'

'No, sir.'

'If it please, Your Worship,' Mary McCarthy intervened.

'Yes, Miss McCarthy?' the judge said, raising his head and looking at her over the rims of his glasses.

'There are a number of witnesses to his character, Your Worship, and they disagree with the view put by Mr Cleeve.'

'But the boy himself has admitted, by implication, that those charges could have had some foundation in the past, if not at present.'

'I know, Your Worship, but our contention is that his misbehaviour in the past was due to certain circumstances and when those circumstances changed, he became an amenable, well-disposed boy.'

'Very well. We shall hear your witnesses in due course. Please go on, Mr Cleeve.'

Mr Cleeve told the judge about Lockie's misdeeds in a number of his foster homes. Lockie had forgotten most of them, and he was enraged by the slant given to them by the lawyer. He shook his head in disbelief as he heard them.

'That's not true!' he shouted and he stood up. Mammy Tallon reached over and rested her hand on his. He closed his mouth again and looked at the judge. The judge was staring at him and there was dead silence in the room for a few moments.

'Are those things not true then, Loughlin?' the judge asked calmly, as if he hadn't noticed Lockie's outburst.

'Sort of true, sir, but he makes them sound a lot different.'

The judge nodded and addressed Mr Cleeve.

'Would you try to humour me, Mr Cleeve. Less of the melodrama, if you please.'

Mr Cleeve apologised, and continued to give details of Lockie's life with foster parents.

'His outrageous behaviour was also evident in his school. If it please, Your Worship, I would like to call a witness to substantiate that.'

'Very well,' the judge said.

Mr Bradley was sent for.

'Mr Bradley,' Mr Cleeve addressed him when he had taken a seat, 'we are trying to get a picture of Loughlin here, so that the judge can decide what is best for him. Could you tell us what you know about him?'

'Yes, of course. He was quiet in the classroom, co-operative really, but seemed to be unpopular with the other boys, and he had a ferocious temper.'

'How's this?' the judge asked. 'You've just said that he was well-behaved in the schoolroom?'

'True, Your Worship. He was quiet enough in the classroom, but I got reports of his violent behaviour in the playground.'

The judge said, 'Well, all right. Tell us about those reports.'

Mr Bradley told about finding Lockie and a companion bruised and bleeding after a brutal fight with a number of boys in the playground. The boys were unanimous in laying the blame on Lockie for the attack.

Miss McCarthy asked if Lockie had given his version of what had happened.

'No,' Mr Bradley said. 'As far as I can remember, he didn't say anything. I assumed his silence meant that he agreed with the account given by the others.'

'How many boys were involved in the fight?'

'I don't know. As I've said, I'm going on what I was told.'

'Did you not think it strange that two boys would take on a large number of others?'

'Well, I don't know how many others there were. If it's the case that they did fight a large number, I think it gives some idea of the viciousness of the two.'

'How is that?'

'Well, it seems they were angry enough to throw caution to the wind, with little regard for the consequences.'

'Could it not also be true that the others picked on them because they were different, Lockie a foster child and his companion a Traveller?'

'I suppose anything is possible.'

'Come on, Mr Bradley, you know young boys pretty well. Is that not a real possibility?'

'Possible yes, but it doesn't square with the account I was given.'

'Which was a one-sided version, as you have already said.'

'Yes.'

The judge gave Miss McCarthy permission to call a witness to the fight in the school yard, and she called Mickey Wheeler. Lockie saw that somebody had tried to tame his wild hair and he was wearing a clean white shirt. Miss McCarthy asked him if he remembered the fight.

'I do, Miss.'

'Tell us about it.'

'You see, Miss, there was these whole lot of fellows calling Lockie names. He wasn't doing nothing to them.'

At this point the judge took over the questioning. He leaned across the table and spoke to Mickey.

'What names were they calling him?' he asked.

'Things like "Boxer", and "Maw Face", and "Muggie", and "Rhino", sir.'

'And did he attack them?'

'No, sir. It was they done the attacking, bumping into him

like, and he standing there by the wall, bothering no one like.'

'And how did you get involved?'

'Well, you see, sir, he was all alone against about ten of them.'

'Was that the only reason you helped him?'

'Ah – no, sir.'

'What other reason had you?'

'Well, you see, sir, he was my friend.'

'Did you win the fight?'

'I'd say 'twas about evens, sir.'

All except Father Shanahan and Mr Cleeve laughed at that. Mr Cleeve did smile a bit, but Father Shanahan just looked down at the table.

Job Diggin, Jim Harrington, and Miss Doolan gave evidence of Pasha's and Mammy Tallon's good character, and also of how well-behaved Lockie was in the time that they knew him.

CHAPTER TWENTY-EIGHT

Cross-Examination

The next witness to be examined was John Farrell. He was given the seat beside Father Shanahan. Mr Cleeve introduced him to the judge and began to question him.

'Would you like to tell the judge about the night you took Loughlin into your home.'

'Aye-aye, Mr Cleeve.'

The judge raised an eyebrow and looked out over his glasses at John Farrell. He made a note on his notebook and looked away again.

'Please address the judge.'

'Well, Judge –'

'Your Worship,' Mr Cleeve corrected.

'Sorry, Worship,' he continued, 'the first night Lockie was in our house, we sent him aloft to his berth at about nine o'clock.'

John Farrell told the story of the knife and the attack on the younger child. Aided by Mr Cleeve's questioning, he made it sound vicious and unprovoked.

When he had finished, Miss McCarthy stood, and without

looking at the witness asked softly, almost as if she were only faintly interested, 'Did you witness the knife attack on Gordon, Mr Farrell?'

'Not exactly,' said Farrell.

He told them that his attention was drawn to the children's room by the cries of the younger child, and his knowledge of what happened was gained from what the young child told him.

'Did you get an account of what happened from Lockie?'

'Yes.'

'Was it the same as the account from the young child?'

'No.'

'Why was it the younger child you believed?'

'Well, I–' he hesitated. 'I knew the younger child. He was already one of our crew. Lockie was a new hand.'

'Now could we come to the time when he was returned to you by gardaí on his second attempt to leave.'

'What's this?' the judge asked. 'Did he run away more than once?'

'He did, Worship, but he wasn't adrift for too long,' Farrell said quickly, as if to assure the judge that it was only a minor setback in their relationship.

'What happened when the guards brought him home?' Miss McCarthy continued.

'Nothing.'

'Did you change his sleeping arrangements?'

'Oh, yes I did,' Farrell shifted uneasily in his chair. 'But I didn't have much choice.'

'Could you tell the judge what his new sleeping arrangements were?'

'Well, I put him aloft in the attic.'

'Had the attic been converted to a bedroom?'

'No.'

'Could you describe it to the judge, then?'

'It was just an ordinary attic, Judge – eh – Your Worship.'

'Was it floored?' Miss McCarthy continued.

'Yes. I had floored it with loose-jointed planks.'

'Did it have a ceiling?'

'No.'

'Just the bare rafters and the roofing felt?'

'Yes, but it was quite comfortable.'

'How was it furnished?'

John Farrell paused and thought about his answer before giving it. 'It didn't have furniture, just a made-up bed for Lockie.'

'Was there anything else up there?'

'We had a lot of stuff there, stored in boxes.' Farrell was obviously becoming uncomfortable under Miss McCarthy's questioning. He raised his voice slightly as he replied, 'Look, you're trying to make out that it was awful, but it wasn't like that at all. It was an all-right berth, ship-shape. Believe me.'

'What lighting had you up there?'

'I didn't have electric light there, but I let him have a candle.'

'And ventilation?'

'There was a skylight.'

'Tell us about access to this eyrie at the top of your house.'

'Miss McCarthy!' the judge rebuked.

'Sorry, Your Worship,' and she turned to John Farrell. 'Tell us about access to the attic?'

'Access?'

'How did you get up and down?'

'A ladder. And through the trapdoor.'

'Was the trapdoor open during the night?'

'No. I closed it when he had gone to bed. That way I knew he'd be safe.'

'Could the trapdoor be opened from the attic?'

'Yes.'

'Easily.'

He hesitated before replying.

'Well, not very easily. You'd need something to grip the battens on the upper side of the door.'

'So, what would have happened if there had been a fire?'

'I'd have gone up and brought him down.'

'And if flames or smoke prevented you from doing that?'

'He could always have got out through the skylight. That was how he got away in the end.'

'Really? Did you have a ladder leaning against the eaves at all times?'

There followed a long silence.

'Have you any more questions, Miss McCarthy?' the judge asked.

'No, Your Worship. I have no more questions for this witness.'

The judge turned to Mr Cleeve: 'If you have no other witnesses, Mr Cleeve, I think we shall recess until after lunch.'

'No other witness as to the boy's character, Your Worship, but I would like to call Father Shanahan later to testify as to the fitness of the Farrell household as a home for this boy.'

CHAPTER TWENTY-NINE

Lockie's Side of the Story

After lunch Miss McCarthy questioned Mammy Tallon. She had asked Pasha beforehand which of them would speak. 'Let Mammy Tallon do it,' Pasha said. 'She is better at the talk than me.'

Miss McCarthy introduced her.

'This is Mrs Underwood, Your Worship, but everyone calls her Mammy Tallon.'

'How did you get such a grand nickname?' the judge asked.

'Pasha called me that,' she said, 'when we first got to know each other.'

The judge seemed very interested in her and Pasha. He continued to question her.

'Pardon me, Miss McCarthy,' he said, 'but I'd like to ask this lady a few questions. I'm curious about these people, about their motive in wanting to care for a twelve-year-old boy, a complete stranger, without any help, financial or other, from any quarter.'

He turned to Mammy Tallon. 'Underwood is an unusual name for a Tallon Islander,' he said.

'Pasha isn't a Tallon Islander. He was born and reared in Coonmore.'

The judge asked her questions about her life on the island, where she had lived before, why they had a house in Coonmore, how she met Pasha and how he got his name.

Lockie was glad that she was the one to do the talking. Pasha was great, but he was a silent kind of man. His answers would have been in one-word grunts.

'All right,' the judge said. 'Go ahead, please, Miss McCarthy.'

'Thank you, Your Worship. Would you tell the judge please, Mammy Tallon, when you first decided you wanted to adopt Lockie.'

'I think it was the first day I saw him, when Dadge brought him to our house.'

'Dadge?' the judge inquired.

'His real name is Paddy Mulcair, Your Worship, but everyone calls him Adagio, Dadge for short.'

'Why did you decide you wanted to adopt him?' Miss McCarthy asked again.

Mammy Tallon thought for a while. 'He looked so lost, so forlorn,' she said eventually. 'My heart went out to him. I think it must have been the sad look in his eyes. He looked like someone who had already lived out a lifetime.'

'He's been with you now for almost a year. Have you changed your mind in the meantime?'

'Oh, no! We want to look after him even more now that we have come to know him.'

'Thank you, Mammy Tallon. That's all my questions, Your Worship.'

Mr Cleeve spoke. 'May I ask a few questions, Your Worship?'

'Yes, go ahead, Mr Cleeve.'

'In all the time you've known him, Mrs Underwood, have you ever seen him in a rage?' Mr Cleeve asked.

'Yes, twice.'

Mr Cleeve was taken aback. He didn't expect that his task would be so easy.

'Please, tell us about it,' he asked eagerly. 'What made him angry? How did he behave when he was angry?'

'The first time I saw him angry was when Dadge brought him to our house and we were wondering what should be done with him. Someone suggested finding his foster parents and sending him back to them.' She looked at Lockie. 'He shouted at us that he would never go back, that if he were sent back, he would run away again. He was so upset.'

'All right,' Mr Cleeve interrupted. 'What about the second time?'

'I've not seen him angry again until yesterday. When you were giving an account of how he behaved in the homes he was in before. I could see the anger rise in him.'

'Oh! Why should that make him angry?'

'What you said would not in itself make him angry because a grain of truth was in it, but your account was twisted, so unfair, that it was hard for him to take.'

Mr Cleeve changed from that line of questioning too. He asked how they could provide for a boy about to begin his secondary education on the mainland.

'We can provide,' Mammy Tallon said quietly.

'How can you? You have scarcely any income other than your husband's dole, and education for someone on the island normally involves boarding on the mainland.'

'As I've already said, we can provide.'

'How can you, Mammy Tallon?' the judge intervened.

'It's important for us to know that.'

'We have put the house in Coonmore up for sale, and it'll be sold in a short time.'

Lockie was flabbergasted. 'No!' he blurted out.

'Why not?' the judge asked.

'It's all they have, that and the house on the island. I don't want them to give that away for me.'

'Then how do you propose your education should be financed, young man?' the judge continued.

'I don't want an education. I just want to stay on the island and go fishing with Pasha and help around.'

'I see. I want to have a word with you later, young man, when these people have finished. Carry on, Mr Cleeve.'

'I have no more questions for this lady, Your Worship.'

'Is that all then?' the judge asked, looking first at Miss McCarthy and then at Mr Cleeve.

'I would just like to make a few points concerning the Farrell family, Your Worship, or rather, I would like to give Father Shanahan the opportunity of making them for me.'

'Very well.'

'Father Shanahan,' Mr Cleeve turned to the priest. 'This application was made at your behest. Why did you feel compelled to seek Lockie's return to the Farrell family?'

Father Shanahan, who had been slouched down in his chair, in deep thought, roused himself and sat upright. He cleared his throat and swallowed. His moment had come.

He delivered his speech to the court in public address mode, as if he were giving a sermon. 'My concern,' he said 'and it is my only concern, is for the moral and religious welfare of this child. Nothing else.

'I am positive that he would be well cared-for in those, and in all other respects, by the devoted, Christian family of

John and Rita Farrell. They can give him everything, a good education, training in social skills, moral formation of the highest standard, and the opportunity to develop his potential to the full. Not alone that, but they can instil Christian principles that will stand to him all his life.

'I must, as a priest, plead with Your Worship to consider the good of this poor child's soul above all other things. John and Rita Farrell will give him everything he needs.'

'Not everything!' Mammy Tallon said quietly.

'What's that? What's that?' the judge said.

Mammy Tallon said nothing.

'What can the Farrells not give him, Mammy Tallon?' the judge persisted.

'Someone that really cares for him!'

The judge broke the long silence that followed Mammy Tallon's remark, 'Have you finished, Father Shanahan?'

'Yes, Your Worship. I have no more to say. I leave the fate of this boy in your capable hands.'

'All right then,' the judge said, gathering his papers together. 'Before I give my decision, I would like to speak to Lockie. In private. Would all others leave the room, please, until I send for you?'

The others rose slowly and moved towards the door.

'Miss Cuneen,' the judge called. 'Would you stay, please?'

CHAPTER THIRTY

The Verdict

The judge turned to Miss Cuneen when the others had gone.

'Nobody thought fit to call you as a witness,' he said. 'What do you think of this young man?'

'I think he is a very intelligent boy,' she said. 'I'm sure he means well, but he is extremely sensitive.'

'And how do you account for his outbursts of rage?'

'He was already eighteen months old when he was abandoned. It is quite probable that a bond had formed between him and his carer, his mother, I presume. To have that bond broken at that time could have left him with a terrible feeling of rejection. That feeling could have remained with him for a long time.'

'Up to the present?' the judge asked.

'Yes, I would think so. He, more than most children of his age, would have been conscious of a wide emotional gulf between him and his foster families.'

'Why more than most?'

'Because he is so intelligent and so sensitive.'

The judge shuffled through some papers on the table.

'I can see from the notes you supplied to the court,' he said, 'that you seem to have got on well with him.'

'Yes. I have always found him agreeable and well-intentioned, but I have found it difficult to find a suitable home for him.'

The judge turned to Lockie. 'Tell me about yourself, Lockie.'

'What will I tell?'

'Tell me about the families you lived with. Do you remember the first one?'

Lockie told him about his life with his foster families, about never feeling as if he belonged. He told about the schools, the name-calling, the bullying, the fighting.

'Was there anything good at all in your life?' the judge asked.

'The first good thing was Mickey Wheeler, but that didn't last long. Then I met Dadge, and he was funny, but I liked him too. After that I met Pasha and Mammy Tallon and that was the best of all.'

'Tell me about it.'

Lockie told about meeting Pasha and Mammy Tallon and going with them through the country, to the funfair, and especially about his life on the island with them. As the story went on, he became less and less fearful, and his account made the judge and Miss Cuneen laugh at times.

The judge had heard enough. 'Would you ask the sergeant to recall the people involved in the case, including all the witnesses, please, Lockie?'

When the others had come into the court room, the judge kept them in suspense for a few moments as he looked around, piercing each one with his bright eyes. The sound of traffic came faintly from the street outside the court house, and, for the first time since the hearing began, Lockie noticed it.

'I have listened very carefully to everything you have said,' the judge began. 'I would like to thank all of you, and to express the court's appreciation of your interest and concern for Lockie's welfare. I, too, am concerned for his welfare, and it is with that in mind that I have arrived at my decision.

'I am particularly appreciative of Father Shanahan's concern for the boy. I have no doubt he acted from the worthiest of motives. I hope, however, that he will forgive me when I say that acting solely on principle can lack that little touch of humanity that can be very important in a child's life.

'I believe that, above all else, a boy like Lockie needs a strong tie of parental affection for his emotional and psychological well-being.'

Lockie noticed that Mammy Tallon's hand was shaking. Pasha was like a stone statue. He didn't look at the judge, but his eyes were lowered, as if he found a spot on the table in front of him of compelling interest.

'I have decided,' the judge continued, 'to turn down Father Shanahan's application.'

Mammy Tallon drew a sharp breath, but Pasha did not change his expression or move his gaze from the table. All the others, except the two lawyers, looked up and held their breath.

'My priority is Lockie's welfare. I have no doubt that that too is your concern, Father Shanahan, and yours, Mr and Mrs Farrell. But it is my firm opinion, from all I have heard, that his welfare is best served by leaving him with Mr and Mrs Underwood on Tallon Island. The boy is obviously happy and well cared for, and there is clearly a mutual feeling of affection there that may have been missing from his life up to now.'

'Has Your Worship considered their age?' Mr Cleeve asked.

'Yes, I have, and while they seem healthy and vigorous at this moment, and I believe there is no reason to think that they won't continue to be so for the next four or five years at least, I must, of course, consider their age.

'Consequently, I have decided to direct the Eastern Health Board to monitor the situation regularly, about twice a year for the next five years. I know that the area is not within their jurisdiction, but I think it would be in the best interest of the boy if the social worker involved were Miss Cuneen. She is the one most familiar with the case. In the event of a change in circumstances or any report of violence or wrong-doing on Lockie's part the Board may apply to have Lockie taken from the Underwood family.

'The allowance for his upkeep will be paid to Mr and Mrs Underwood by the Southern Health Board, as he will be living in their area. Once again, thank you all for your contributions.'

The judge gathered his papers and put them in a folder. The people around the table reacted in different ways to the decision. Mammy Tallon was smiling broadly. Pasha looked at the judge, but his expression did not change. Lockie knew, however, that he was glad. Miss Cuneen smiled. The priest's head was lowered, so it was impossible to know what he was thinking, and the lawyers gave no sign of their feelings.

As they went along the corridor towards the main waiting-room, the priest came to Mammy Tallon and Pasha and offered his hand.

'Forgive me if I made trouble for you,' he said, 'but I was acting for the good of the boy, as I saw it. I hope he prospers in your care. From what I've heard in there, I think the judge may be right. You can give the boy the kind of affection that he might not get anywhere else.'

Lockie went into the waiting-room with his new mother and father, and they were mobbed by their friends, asking what the decision was.

Pasha told them. 'Lockie's coming home with us,' he said, and it was as if all present had been touched by electricity. Their faces lit up with gladness and they showered congratulations on Lockie.

They left the court house, and Lockie went down the street with Mickey and Tom to where their van was parked. They said goodbye. A new life was dawning for Lockie, and Mickey was going back to his old life on the road. As the van drove away, Mickey put his head out the window and waved. They had said nothing about meeting again.

Lockie, Dadge, Pasha and Mammy Tallon had tea and sandwiches in a café in the main street. They did some shopping, and then headed for the pier at Barrymore. Pasha's boat was moored there. Mammy Tallon thought Lockie should have a few days off school to give him time to recover from his ordeal and to celebrate the verdict. She and Pasha decided that he should go back to the island with them and stay until the following Monday.

'Will you not come with us?' Mammy Tallon invited Dadge.

'No, thank you very much, Mammy Tallon,' Dadge said. 'I must be on my way. I'll tell you something though. I wouldn't mind taking up your offer around Christmas again.'

'You'll be more than welcome. You know that,' Pasha told him.

'Good! Good! Christmas is a lonely time on the road, and cold too. I'll see ye all around Christmas so. Good luck to ye now, Lockie boy, you're in luck.'

'I know that, Dadge.'

Pasha cast off, and, as they left the harbour, Lockie looked back. Dadge was standing on the pier waving, and Lockie waved back. They were soon out of the harbour and heading south-west towards the island.

Mammy Tallon sat in the bow, rising up and falling down as they rode the crests and hollows of the waves. Lockie was sitting on the thwart just behind her, and Pasha sat at the stern, holding the tiller to keep her steady, as she faced into the wind.